THE GIRL

in the

RED CAPE

THE GIRL

in the

RED CAPE

A MYSTICAL SLED RIDE

Written by SUZY DAVIES
Illustrated by MICHELE BOURKE

The Girl in The Red Cape: A Mystical Sled Ride

Published in 2019.

This is a work of fiction. Names, characters, places and incidents either are products of the author's imagination or are used fictitiously. Any resemblance to actual events or locales or persons, living or dead, is entirely coincidental.

I.S.B.N: 9781699286098

TABLE OF CONTENTS

AUTHOR DEDICATIONS

Once upon a time, a mother sat at a sewing machine, red velvet, satin and silver buttons on the table. She worked and worked. In a day and a night she had made it—a red cape for her very own "Little Red Riding Hood." A small girl wanted something to wear for a children's fancy dress party. This book is dedicated to the memory of this remarkable woman: artist, dressmaker, dancer, singer, gardener, swimmer, crusader, lover of children—my mother, Joan.

This book is also dedicated to young people and adults all over the world who believe in the power they have inside themselves to make secret wishes and dreams come true.

ILLUSTRATOR DEDICATIONS

Firstly, I'd like to dedicate this book to all of my grandchildren, who inspire me daily with their imagination. Also I dedicate this book to my Mum, from whom I get my love of painting. To all the children and young at heart, who will feel inspired by this book, to pick up a paint brush or pen to create their own fairytale.

I'd also like to dedicate this book to all the great artists that have inspired me, and will continue to do so in the future.

ILLUSTRATOR ACKNOWLEDGEMENTS

I'd like to begin by thanking Suzy Davies, author, for believing in me and my work, and for realising my dreams to illustrate a children's book. I'd also like to thank Alfie, George, Oscar and all of my grandchildren. For all their help with their secret messages within these pictures and for helping me see through a child's eye.

I'd also like to take the time to thank my daughter Amy and my friend, David, for their practical help and encouragement.

Special thank you to everyone at my local art shop, for their friendship, encouragement and endless supplies.

AUTHOR ACKNOWLEDGEMENTS

First and foremost, my heartfelt gratitude goes to Michele Bourke, illustrator for this book. She has a wonderful feel for interpretation, a keen sense of color, and that is why I think of her as "The Fabulous M." Her natural gifts inspire me.

I wish to thank Champion Musher, Winner of The Junior Iditarod, 2019, Anna Stephan, for all her advice, expertise and help in creating our story. It is greatly appreciated!

Many thanks to my husband, Craig, for hearing our story from start to finish, for encouraging me, and for spurring me on. He helps me to have faith in my abilities.

I wish to thank those who read my books for their loyal support—all my friends, fans and fellow authors.

Finally, a big "Thank You" to Jesse Gordon for the excellent job formatting this book.

CHAPTER ONE

The Red Cape

Far, far away, in a place known as Alaska, darkness was beginning to fall. A man was walking across the vast wilderness. He made slow progress. His dog pulled on the leash as if she knew they were almost there. They were headed for Anchorage. The dog, a fur ball of energy, kept her nose to the ground. She moved fast as if something was driving her forward, some kind of reward or prize.

But on that night, all they were doing was travelling. They followed an old familiar path, man and dog, leaving their footprints in the snow. The man stopped. The dog, who had a black-grey and white coat, looked round. But the man's eyes followed the shafts of warm light that played across the white landscape, illuminating snow-drenched trees that surrounded the log cabin nearby.

As if to gather strength, the man signalled his dog with the leash. The two moved forward, climbing a snowy bank. They arrived on a pathway, a foot or so below the chalet window.

In the window, was the dark outline of a woman at work. She was sitting at a trestle table, turning the wheel of a sewing machine. Then, as the light grew dim, she stood near the window, her nimble fingers taking in the fabric, a stitch here, another there. In the twilight, no colour was visible, except the warm glow that came through the glass.

The man stopped again. This time, his gaze flew toward the heavy door. The dog whined with excitement, tugged on the leash, then stopped to sniff the snow. The man moved toward the house, appeared to stay a few moments, as if in deep thought. Then, he leaned a stick against the side that faced west. His eyes looked further down the path again. The snow was beginning to dance under the darkening skies. He must press on.

Inside the cabin, Mrs. Chapman sewed and sewed, unawares.

Around midnight, she smiled and gave a heavy sigh. The red cape was ready. But she would not call and wake Stella.

Quite soon, she would tell her the secret. Mrs. Chapman put away her work in the long wooden chest in her bedroom. For a few minutes, she peered through the frosty glass of her bedroom window, watching the snow tumble, earthwards. Then, the last drop of light was squeezed out from the ink black sky.

"Then, as the light grew dim, she stood near the window, her nimble fingers taking in the fabric, a stitch here, another there."

CHAPTER TWO
The Alaskan Inuk

Tom, The Inuk, pressed on. With only his dog and the faint glimmer of torchlight to guide him, he made quick progress across the tundra, a few miles on. Snow was blowing, wind-wards. The powder swirled, like white dust from the cosmos, about his head and feet. His dog, Sesi, nosed forward. They reached a clearing in a wooded area, where, camouflaged amongst the trees, was a tent.

Tom lit a fire. And he began to work on a dream-catcher. It was made from lightweight wood, ribbons of rainbow material, and birds' feathers. As he worked, in his mind's eye, he saw two children, Billy and Stella, his step-brother and step-sister.

He would make two dream-catchers, one for each of them. Even though they were raised very differently from how he grew up, it was a good thing. They combined some of the Eskimo traditions—the old ways —with the ways of the modern world. Alaska belonged to them. It was their heritage. These children would do their parents proud.

"These dream-catchers will protect my brother and sister from entities who roam the wilderness, and steal away their dreams," he whispered.

"These dream-catchers will protect my brother and sister from entities who roam the wilderness, and steal away their dreams."

And the wind answered—a chill wind that blew up, settling powder on his eyebrows and eyelashes. The flames of the fire fanned into the wings of a raven bird.

"Ah! It's you, is it?" Tom said.

The bird was watching him.

"Please, Raven, er Black-Claw, take these dream-catchers to Eva—they are for the kids."

The bird peered at his handiwork, and back again at Tom.

"I know you!"

Tom gave the raven three berries for his trouble.

Up, up and away, the raven took the dream-catchers. The wind was against him, and sped him on his route.

In the morning, for Tom, a short journey on to Anchorage lay ahead. He planned to take his wood carvings, paintings and dream-catchers to an old customer, Mac, who ran a tourist shop. Visitors were coming in. Hotels all over Anchorage would be packed. It was racing season, after all!

In the silence that surrounded him, Tom's thoughts travelled to his mother, Ariana. Harsh words had come between them, a few years ago. How many times had he crossed her path? How many times had he feared her tongue? It was all a misunderstanding. One of life's trials, when two worlds crossed and clashed. He breathed in the cold air and sighed.

His dog, Sesi, lay beside him, her mesmeric blue eyes beaming out of her white-grey face, like sapphires in the snow. He patted her on the head. He was glad he had her. Named after the landscape in which she was born, she came from a long line of champion sled dogs who served the mushers well.

"I'll meet you in Anchorage!"

These words echoed through Tom's brain that was now in a whirl of excited energy.

The dog sensed Tom's excitement. She rose, licked Tom's face, and circled round him three times.

Tom understood. He reached inside the tent and drew out a piece of fresh boned salmon. He divided it into two portions.

Minutes later, the fire crackled up into a plume of smoke. It spat and hissed, Tom all the while turning the morsels on two hand-made skewers.

Sesi whined and slobbered at the jowls. Tom laughed, took Sesi's charcoal-burnt salmon off the wood stick to cool, then tossed it on the ground.

The two of them ate together, comfortable, in each other's company. They munched the fish in unison, yet neither of them said a word.

After their meal, Tom shuffled snow onto the fire. And they both sat, gazing up at the Skyworld. It looked like a giant ink-black cape that let in chinks of light—windows to their Earth. From these windows, ancient spirits gazed upon them and protected them.

"In time, in time, all will be all right again, won't it, Sesi!"

Sesi nuzzled Tom's ankles.

The two entered the tent on all fours, and very soon man and dog were asleep—Tom sprawled out on his back, Sesi at his feet. A big journey lay ahead.

CHAPTER THREE

Eva's

"How long till we get to Mom's?" Stella said. She tightened the toggles on her hood to bring it closer to her face.

"It's a good way, yet."

Billy gave Pakak a "Whoa!" which meant, "Slow Down!"

He glanced round, and in the distance he saw, silhouetted on the horizon, an undulating line of wild creatures, moving together. The wolves were on their scent!

"We'd better not go through the wood," he shouted, "that's the long way round!"

"O.K!"

"Make haste!" cried Billy. "There are wolves!"

"What?"

"I said, wolves!"

"You're serious?" Stella frowned. So, this wasn't one of his pranks. She clutched her throat.

"Make haste n' we'll lose 'em!"

"Are we crossing the river, then?" Stella said. She struggled to raise her voice.

"Yep, don't worry!" Billy shouted back.

"D'ya hear me?"

Billy looked round again.

Stella, whose face was as pallid as ivory, gave a quiet signal, "Hike!" With that, the sled dogs all picked up speed.

Miles and miles they went, the sleds swishing across the snow, the dogs' paws flying so fast they were almost airborne.

As they approached the river, they crossed an area of land which still had ancient gnarled tree roots. Green and malevolent, they rose out of the snow, like bitter snares.

Icebergs were floating up the river, northwards, swirling in the current like spinning-tops.

"How can we cross?" Stella thought.

They saw a lone wolf, drifting on an iceberg further up. All of a sudden, it leapt into the air, and landed on the opposite bank. It shook its body. The freezing water flew in all directions. The wolf loped ahead of them, disappearing into a wood.

"How can we cross the river?" Billy was thinking.

As if by magic, a whirlwind hit the water; it froze, making a narrow path of black ice.

But Yurairia was up for the challenge. She showed the other dogs how to dance over any obstacle and float over thin ice.

Miska, Billy's smallest dog, shivered and whined. She hesitated on the bank.

Pakak rose to the challenge and pushed her on. They slid forwards, with the lightest touch of their paws. The sleds rattled as they skidded across the ice. Any weight, and the ice would not hold.

"Steady! Steady!" Billy said, while Stella coaxed her dogs in a soft, gentle voice that was almost a whisper. They understood what she meant.

At the last minute, the dogs were airborne. One leap, and they heaved the children and the sleds onto solid ground.

But still the wolf-pack were on their trail.

"We'll catch em!" the King Wolf said, flashing his teeth in anger.

"Remember, we have scores to settle."

The pack stood together and howled their call to action.

"Listen! Did you hear that?"

"We must hurry!"

The wolves had decided to take the longer route; they knew where Stella and Billy were going. Many times, these watchers had viewed them from a distance. Although the wolves were taking the longer route, they had the advantage. Ah, yes!

Still further, the children and dogs went. A storm was coming in. Snow swirled in the air in circular movements, stinging the children's faces, pinching the dogs' noses.

Stella drew in her hood still closer to her face. It ached with the cold.

"Alright, Stella?" Billy said, trying to smile.

He knew this was all good training for what lay ahead of them in the Junior Race. He hoped she had it in her.

Hours and hours, these young mushers journeyed.

A solitary travelling man cupped his ears as he heard the cries of the dogs approaching their destination. He tilted his head. Was it dogs or wolves? He could not tell. He shook his head, stamped his snow-shoes, shifted his backpack, and dug his carved stick with the family crest of a raven into the snow. It was going to be a long night ahead.

As for Stella and Billy, they were passing the edge of the wood, when the same wolf they saw near the river came towards them. Billy froze and Stella cowed away. The dogs stalled the sleds. But, with their piercing eyes fixed on the wolf, they stood their ground. The wolf gazed back at them with dark soulful eyes, and loped off into the distance, in the direction of their grandmother's house.

The last hundred yards of their journey seemed the longest.

When they reached the cabin yard, Billy tethered the sleds to nearby trees with snub lines. He stomped his feet as if to say, "We've made it!"

"Blood-curdling wolf howls and dog snarls pierced the air."

But, in the periphery of her vision, Stella glimpsed an animal lurking in the bushes. She emerged nose first, and sniffed the air. It was the lone wolf!

"How gentle your eyes look!" Stella said.

"A good way to show how kind I am," the wolf replied.

"But your nose is very big, Mrs. Wolf!" Billy said.

"It's my way of knowing when dinner's done!" Lone Wolf replied.

"What huge legs you have, Mrs. Wolf," came a voice.

But it was neither Billy nor Stella! Oh, No! It was King Wolf, who suddenly sprang out at them! He signalled to the others.

"My legs have served me well!" cried Lone Wolf. "I can run with the best of 'em!"

All at once, the pack lurched forward. As if by magic, the dogs ran free.

Akiak, Stella's dog, who was known for her bravery, stared out the King Wolf as if to say, "Leave us alone!"

And Pakak, who was Billy's, was game for a challenge. He bared his teeth, going for the neck of the wolf leader. He attacked the tender part near the jugular. King Wolf lashed out with his claws. He towered on his hind legs. He was a giant! But the dog-pack all lunged forward. Every sinew, every muscle, moved together like a well-oiled machine.

Fur was flying! Blood-curdling wolf howls and dog snarls pierced the air.

Dogs and wolves drew blood.

Miska or Little Bear, as she was known, took on a wolf twice her size. It tore into her front leg. She let out a high-pitched yelp! Now, she was lame. Stella froze, the sting of tears in her eyes. Billy bit his bottom lip.

But Mrs. Lone Wolf just stood her ground with a stare that unsettled all enemies.

The children watched as one by one, the wolves, defeated, sloped off into the dense clearing. But, amidst the scuffle, they never saw where Mrs. Wolf, the lone wolf, went.

The silence after the battle was eerie. All they could hear was the "Pick, Pok, Puk" of snow as if fell to the earth.

Snow soon covered all traces of blood that were on the ground. It was as if nothing had ever happened; the wolves were gone, the lone wolf had disappeared. The only sign that a war was won was a lame snow-dog.

Billy put his arm round Stella, who was sobbing.

"It's O.K."

He gathered up Miska, and set her down under the tree.

Stella gave him a questioning look.

"I have an idea," Billy said. "Have you a knife . . . ?"

Right away, brother and sister got to work.

Billy tore off his jacket, and laid it on the sled. Then, he ripped the arm off his shirt.

Stella dragged down a tree-branch. She took a knife out of her pocket. Her deft hands worked away until the wood was smooth and straight.

Billy wrapped the splint against Miska's wounded leg, twisting the shirt sleeve round and round, then up and round the dog's neck to make a kind of sling. When he had finished, he took little Miska in his arms and carried her towards the door.

Stella lifted the door latch. The other dogs followed them inside. Billy settled them in the kitchen, while Stella called out, "Grandma, are you there?"

"Come in, my dear," said Mrs. Wolf.

The bedroom door was half-open. As Stella peeped inside and entered, a shaft of rainbow light illuminated her way. She beckoned Billy.

What a sight awaited them!

They couldn't believe it—how different their Grandma Eva looked!

Propped up in bed, glasses slipping down her nose, she was reading a book. Stella recognised the cover illustration. It reminded her of a fairy tale her nan read to her when she was just a girl.

"Grannie-Can-Do?" Stella smiled.

"You bet!" Lone Wolf said.

"Now, don't laugh!" the wolf grinned, showing a fine set of wolf-like gnashers. "I'm still young at heart, and who doesn't enjoy a fairytale, eh?"

The children exchanged a glance. Billy knotted his eyebrows, and said,

"So, Grandma! Tell us our mom's name!"

"Well, now," said the wolf. "That'd be Ariana!"

"Correct!" Billy said, unsmiling. He imagined he was Mr. Brindley from his senior school.

"And how about my birthday?" whispered Stella, wide-eyed.

"Now then, my pretty little Sagittarius. Let me see!"

At this point, Grandma Wolf peered over her glasses. Then, her eyes looked up, in thought.

"You were born on a very cold night! Ah, I remember it as if it was yesterday! The sky was so dark, and clear! Such a starry night, and cloudless, it was.

Let me see now. It was on 7th of December! Your mom was in labour for nearly two days. 7th December. Seven in the evening. Seven's the magic number. Yes, that's it!"

Stella giggled and Billy nudged her. Stella covered her mouth. Billy shifted his weight from one foot to the other.

In a big voice Billy said, "Mrs. Wolf, er, um, I mean, Grannie-Can-Do, I think we'll sleep in the kitchen tonight!"

"Oh, my dear! I had the spare rooms all made up for you . . ."

"What we mean is, the dogs have another long journey in the morning . . . and Miska is sick," Stella said.

Mrs. Wolf nodded, closed the story book with a heavy thump, and said,

"Ah, I'm so sorry about that. We'll see what we can do, eh? You didn't forget your old gran, then. Well, you know, I kept telling myself, must see those little kids soon! I always look out for you, you know!"

The children exchanged a second furtive glance, bid Grannie-Can-Do, "Goodnight!" and closed her door behind them.

*"Propped up in bed, glasses slipping down her nose,
she was reading a book."*

Billy checked on Miska, who was already asleep.

"She will not be able to race," he said to himself. *"She can stay at the house and keep Gran company when Tag is out and about."*

One dog down, maybe his chances of taking part were ruined. But Billy put his own feelings aside. He must look out for Stella! How she had grown. His little sis. But was she up to it? He secretly had his doubts. How disappointed Billy felt; he was the champion racer! His heart belonged among Nature, with his dogs.

As if Tag knew what Billy was thinking, he tapped the door with his nose, like a domestic dog. He wanted to go out. After all, he was a fox.

Billy and Stella wanted to stay and comfort Miska. How well the children slept that night, huddled in the middle of their pack of dogs who kept them safe and warm!

Tag, meanwhile, was doing his nightly watch. He watched the yard and the little copse of trees nearby. Mysterious liquid shadows seemed to move under the trees. And on the wind, he heard the call of the wild.

CHAPTER FOUR

Ariana

Very early, just as the sun was beginning to rise, Ariana held the red
cape up to the window, and smiled. How she had hugged the secret
close to her. She had told no-one, only The Shaman!

An expert seamstress, Ariana's works of art were the talk of the village!
She could sew with no pattern, making a dress or pants for the women folk
in one day. Her method was always the same: find a style that suited her
client, choose the fabric with her client, cut the pieces, skip the tacking
stage altogether, pin it here or there, and machine the fabric. It took one or
two fittings at the most, and Abracadabra—there it was—the perfect fit!
Of course, for this secret creation, the cape of ruby red, Ariana already
knew the measurements. No, No! Stella's big surprise would come, but
not yet!

The mark of Ariana Chapman's work was attention to detail. With a
keen eye for colour, her garments always complemented the wearer—the
tone of their skin, the colour of their eyes. Tom, her son, was the one who
most took after her. He worked with his hands. This artistic inclination
came out in different ways, that's all.

Tom was the sensitive one. But here's where they differed. He never fitted into the hunting scene at all. He had never killed an animal with his

own hands for its pelt. In defence of himself, who knows? He may have done. But now, he stubbornly refused to carry on the hunting traditions of their ancestors. Yet, here was the irony—rumour had it that the wolves, who had their own language, their own understanding of people, regarded him as the one who had slain Queen Wolf because of her striking fur. That is why the Chapman family were plagued by misfortune. The Shaman had told her. And she was the best of them all!

"Ah, then, Stella. Grandma's making sure she's safe, bless her!"

A tiny package had arrived this very morning. Tom must have left it. Next to the package was a walking stick from Eva. He had propped it up against the side of the house. He had carved the family emblem onto it— the face of a raven. What a strange one, her son, Tom! He had left home early. And now, he was such a loner. He was not one for the company of people. Why didn't he knock. Why, like some kind of ghost, had he passed by, without a word? Ariana thought these thoughts, alone in her room. She picked up his photograph. Her artistic, conical hands traced the carved frame and she sighed.

Time was slow today. That was the thing. When you wanted something to happen now, it always dragged the hands of the clock. Time was capricious; when you needed Time it laughed at you. It won the race, leaving you at the starting post.

"Not long, now," Ariana thought, *"and now for Eva's little gift..."*

She opened the little white package, with her name and address written in calligraphy, with swirls about the A and C that made her look more important than she was. Inside the violet wrapping paper was a small silver button. The edge of the button was raised, and there was a fine groove all the way round like a sewing spool.

"Mother is the one, in this family," Ariana muttered with a shake of her head and a smile.

And she took a pen and paper and in her spidery writing wrote:

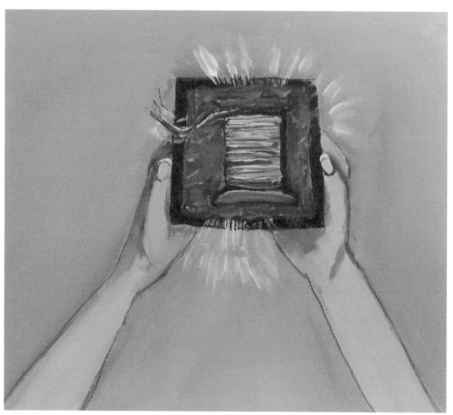

"Inside the violet wrapping paper was a small silver button. The edge of the button was raised, and there was a fine groove all the way round like a sewing spool."

Dearest Mom,

Thank you for the silver button. Got it today! Tom left it! I'll sew it into the cape lining like you said. Weather worse again. Lines down. Expecting Stella and Billy later. Tell them I have a surprise for them.

Don't work too hard. I worry about you!

Did you try the tea I sent you yet?

Hope this reaches you safely.

Love, Ariana X

Just as she signed her letter, Ariana heard a scuttling noise outside. She opened the door.

"Ah! Tag!"

She attached the envelope to the fox's message-collar, fed him some herring from her breakfast table, patted him on the head like a pet dog, and sent him on his way.

"Tag, Hey, Tag! Be careful!" she called after him, snickering.

Tag stopped and pricked up his ears. Then, he bounded off at full tilt, skidding down the snowy bank in the direction of the alpine wood and the shaman's house.

CHAPTER FIVE

Morning at Eva's

Very late in the morning, little Tag nosed at the door, which made a light tapping sound. Mrs. Wolf let her fox in. He was carrying a message in his collar. The cream envelope had spidery writing in midnight blue ink.

"That's good," Mrs. Wolf said, in a murmur.

Tag waited at her heels and stood quite still while she took the envelope.

"Thank you, Tag."

"Must get to bed!"

Soon, Tag was fast asleep.

"Rise and shine!" Mrs. Wolf called in the softest of wolf-voices.

Minutes later, the children were washed, dressed and eating porridge with sticky syrup, washed down with cups of tea. It was such a cosy cabin!

"More porridge? There's plenty!"

Stella waved her hand, "No, um, er, Gran, we're full!"

Gran nodded, but she said nothing. Her magnetic eyes searched their faces. Sometimes, the gaze seemed soft and familiar.

Billy cleared his throat.

"Er, Gran."

"Yes, Billy?" Mrs. Wolf said, cradling the tea-pot in her large hands.

"We want to know, we'd like to know, why did you change into a wolf, and won't we ever see your face, I mean, your human face, again?"

"Well, I knew you'd say that," the wolf said, pouring a second cup of Earl Grey and handing it to Stella.

"Now we all know each other, what am I saying? I can tell you what will happen—at least, you know, some of it, anyway."

Billy gazed into the wolf's eyes as if to say, "Can I trust you?" but before he could speak, the wolf went on . . .

"I have to change back to Grannie-Can-Do in a few minutes because I have some errands to do in the village. The wolves have gone now, so no need to be in disguise, eh! You start getting your things ready because I'll be a long time. Before you go, you'll see my old face again!"

"We prefer Grannie to the wolf," Stella said simply.

"Well, you won't say that to me when you're in the race, now. I'm certain of that! I can run with the best of 'em. If you're in any danger, I'll always be there for you. But one thing about magic. It's only there for you if you believe in it. And it's you that makes the magic happen!"

"We DO believe in you, Gran, er, Mrs. Wolf," Stella said.

"Well, don't forget your old Gran is a very wise woman," Mrs. Wolf said with a flash of her soulful eyes.

Mrs. Wolf put down her cup, and made her way to the bathroom.

Billy and Stella looked at each other.

"I think we're going to have a long wait."

"Ha! That's funny, coming from you!" Billy replied.

Stella wandered into Mrs. Wolf's bedroom; the door was still half-open.

On the dresser, was a cream envelope, the address in dark blue ink, written in a familiar hand. So perhaps she could trust Wolf Gran after all.

*"Yes, Billy?" Mrs. Wolf said, cradling
the tea-pot in her large hands."*

"We should not judge by appearances," thought Stella. *"Time shows us who we can trust. Then, folks show us their true natures. There's nothing worse than false friends who lead us by the hand into all kinds of dangers. They have two sides—one light, one dark. Nothing's unusual about that. But false friends take us from our true paths. I'd rather have honest enemies or rivals. They challenge us and shape us. They help us more than they know. They give us courage—something to go against."*

At these thoughts, Stella Honor Chapman laughed out loud. Her strength and her weakness was her imagination. It took her soaring the skies, plummeting to the depths. What was real, and what was fantasy? She wanted to explore life's secrets and mysteries, unravel all the threads, know what life meant.

There Stella sat on Gran's bed. On the quilt, was the story book, *"Little Red Riding Hood."* She peeped inside it, saw the girl, familiar to her, with the bright red cape. She was standing next to a woman just like kind old Gran. Stella reclined against the pillows, daydreaming for what seemed like hours.

A faint shadow played across the glass. Stella stirred from the bed. She stood at the window, gazing at the snow, which sparkled like silver. How peaceful it was! And how quiet, like a dream! Then, with a soft tap at the door, an old woman appeared.

CHAPTER SIX

Revelations!

The door creaked as Stella opened it to see the old woman. Well, of all things, it was Gran again!

"Gran!" said Stella, giving her a huge kiss on the side of her face.

"Grannie-Can-Do!" Billy said with a huge grin.

Even though they were independent and making their own way in life, Billy and Stella always thought of lovable Gran as "Grannie-Can-Do." She made the best of any situation. She made things happen.

"Phew! That was close. Those wolves. Acting like they own the place!"

It was a narrow escape, but Grannie made it to the village and back.

Of course, Gran, Billy and Stella knew that the wolves did own the place, Alaska, that beautiful wilderness that was their home. Living side by side with nature was a delicate balance.

"Now, how about another cup of your Gran's tea and some ginger biscuits, eh?"

Gran winked as she took off her coat and put it over the chair.

Brother and sister nodded in unison.

"Well, I guess you'll be on your way in a minute or two, so I have something to tell you before you go!"

"We're not going yet!" said Billy.

"Ah! That's good. I don't get to see enough of you both, these days!"

Gran stroked Tag, who was drowsy. He wobbled to his feet, then sat down again in his bed.

The children continued drinking tea.

"Tag here is going to help you in the race. Isn't that right, Tag?"

The fox pricked up his ears and jumped!

He tore round the room, his claws skidding on the wooden floor as if he was doing a victory lap.

"Now settle down, Tag! Watch where you're going!"

Billy laughed and dunked another biscuit. His sister snickered behind her hand.

Tag took no notice. But when he had run out of energy, he returned to his bed.

"As I was saying," Gran said, "this little fella has a big heart and likes helping people. Well, you know, when it gets very dark, and when the snow fills the sky and you can't see your way, Tag here is the expert!"

At this point, Gran leaned back in her chair and cackled.

Although they couldn't be quite sure what she meant, Billy and Stella joined in.

"An' another thing," Gran said, leaning forward. "Your mom has a gift waiting for you, Stella, when you arrive. An' Billy—your mom hasn't forgotten you—there's a present for you as well! Tom helped. These gifts will help you in the race! And there are more things right here for both of you, that Raven brought!"

At this point, Billy and Stella both put their cups down. They were like scary twins, exchanging quick glances in a "you've spooked us" kind of way—grinning and scowling at the same time.

"Do you believe in your dreams? I hope you do! You should guard them with all your heart. Never let anyone tell you they are nonsense!"

Gran poured refills from the teapot.

*"It was a narrow escape, but Grannie
made it to the village and back."*

"Now what was I saying . . . Oh my . . . I had it on the tip of my tongue and now . . ." She spoke in a teasing voice.

"Oh, Gran! Tell us, p-please," Stella said, slurping the last drop of her tea.

"Ah! It's come back to me. Wait a minute!"

With that Gran scurried quite fast, the inquisitive fox in pursuit, and they both disappeared behind the half-open bedroom door.

The children heard a rolling sound. It was the dressing table drawer opening and closing.

Then, Gran reappeared, Raven perched on her shoulder. She was holding something in her hands behind her back.

"Close your eyes!"

Billy closed his eyes, but Stella's eyelids twitched.

"Stella, no cheating!"

Stella closed her eyes—properly this time.

"O.K. Let's count to seven, the magic number!"

On seven, Gran sang, "Ta, Dah!" and produced two rainbow dreamcatchers that shimmered with dancing lights.

"Aw, Gran, they're beautiful!" Stella said, putting her hands together close to her chest.

"Thanks, Gran!" said Billy matter-of-factly in the kind of gruff voice that was halfway between boyhood and manhood. What were dreamcatchers for? He couldn't imagine!

"Are they just for decoration?" he said. He held his dreamcatcher up to the light and examined it.

"Yes, Billy, they are for decoration but they're also part of our Alaskan Inuit traditions! They're magical! Only pleasant dreams come through these threads!"

"That's right, Gran, they keep evil spirits at bay," said Stella studying the eyes of the wolf. "Did you make them?" she added.

"What were dreamcatchers for? He couldn't imagine!"

"No, Tom did!" Gran said. "He heard you are taking part in the junior race, and he's so excited for you both!"

"Maybe I won't," announced Billy, his eyes fixed on the floor.

"Never say never," Gran replied. "Now, little Miska here! I'll look after her. I think Tom has a plan. But you'll have to ask him what it is! No, Tom never was one for the hunting. I don't know why the wolves think such terrible things about one so gentle. Anyway, he keeps busy with his art . . . Never mind, I'll tell you when you're a little older . . ."

The family was full of secrets! Why couldn't they just say them, plainly and simply. It was the women! Why did they always have to make everything a mystery? It was different from how Billy saw the world.

Stella was thinking the opposite! Gran made everything a mystery. And there was nothing in the world more beautiful than mysterious things. Stella thought about the wolves. All they were doing was following their instincts for survival. She believed they had their own Alaska, their own wolf-stories about how they found the land before it was ever discovered. She gave them their space. But sometimes, she wondered how they lived side by side with man. She wanted to help them.

"Stella, Stella!" Gran clicked her fingers and Stella broke out of her trance.

"What were you thinking, Love?"

"Nothing, Gran!"

Stella's gaze met her Gran's gaze, and in that moment, Gran was Wolf Mother.

CHAPTER SEVEN

The Red Cloak and The Carved Wand

"Ariana, Ariana!" came the dramatic voice down the line. "At last! Where have you been?"

"Oh, I've been doing a bit of this and that," said Ariana with an air of mystery.

"Are they with you yet?"

Ariana moved to the window.

"Yes! I can see them. You didn't tell me the raven was coming, too!"

"Well, you know what they say about the flight of the crow? It's always the most direct route. And ravens are part of that family. Some say they are even smarter than crows, and I've seen it with my own eyes!"

"But sleds don't fly!"

"That's true. But Black-Claw can keep the children safe by flying ahead to spot any danger!"

"Good thinking, Mom."

"Thanks, I do try. Now this magic . . . the silver button, I mean. That's important! Did you sew it into the cloak-lining?"

"Yes, Mom!"

"That's good. Now you must tell Stella what to do. Don't mention anything about magic to Billy. He doesn't believe in it, yet! He'll have to see, later, with his own eyes. I'll send him a voice-thought when he needs it. Between you and I, that wand you're going to give him's magical. Now here's how it works . . ."

"Cool!" breathed Ariana, when Eva had explained everything. "It's so cool!"

"Oh, glad you like the idea. Now, Love, I think it's best if the kids go through the wood with the sleds—it's the shortest route as the crow flies. They need to head south—Black-Claw'll show them. Then they can catch the train to Anchorage. Tom's looking forward to seeing them again! We've talked. It's been a long time!"

Just as Gran spoke these words, the raven tapped on the door. Two pink noses pressed up against the windows, and tapped lightly on the misty glass.

"Gotta go, Mom! They're here!"

"Thank goodness!" exclaimed Eva. "I can always rely on my Black-Claw!"

"Bye, Love!"

"Bye, Mom!

"Speak soon!"

"Take care! Love to the children!"

Ariana put down the receiver and went to the door.

"Hey!"

"Mom!"

Billy stomped his feet on the snowy front step. Stella took off her fleece hat and shook it.

"Boy, it's cold today!" Stella said, catching her breath.

Ariana stepped out and stared at the sky. It was almost twilight. The sun dipped slowly like a tangerine, melting into the skyline.

Together brother and sister stepped inside. It was so late. Yet, they were full of energy. Stella's eyes shone with anticipation. Billy looked more animated than usual. Somehow, he was less serious. Perhaps the danger of the short journey was now lifted.

The two took off their gloves, and hung their jackets on the brass hooks in the hallway. They toasted their hands by the open fire.

Stella spotted a piece of ruby red material and thread on the sewing table.

"Been busy?" she said with a casual air.

"Maybe!" said Ariana in a rising tone. "Are you two hungry? I have fresh salmon on the grill if you'd like some!"

"Yes, please, Mom!"

"Sit down, then! Go on, help yourselves! When we've finished, I have a big surprise, for both of you!"

They ate the meal in silence.

Billy and Stella cleared the table and did the chores between them. Ariana disappeared into the next room.

"What's the surprise? Do you know?"

Billy shrugged his shoulders and put his finger over his mouth. "Sh! She's here!" he whispered as Ariana reappeared.

"You know," said Ariana. "Whatever happens in this big race, I am proud I've raised such good kids. I mean, you're not kids anymore, really. More young adults. I want you to know that I'm proud of you, win or lose. There are no losers in the end, because it's a great honour that you were chosen for the race! Both of you, mind! That's double the honour!"

Billy blushed and looked at the floor. How he hated it when his face was all hot and looked like a beetroot. Stella twirled a lock of red hair round and round her index finger.

Eva pretended not to notice. Although privately, it took her back to when she was young and unsure. Motherly love flowed over her features like a gentle light illuminating a hidden path. Her eyes softened and the ends of her mouth suggested a faint smile.

"What's the surprise, Mom?" Stella, who was feeling more confident, said.

"Wait a minute!" said Ariana, going into her bedroom to get the cloak and the wand from the treasure chest.

Then, after a few minutes that seemed like hours, she emerged with one gift in each hand.

Stella's first glimpse was bright fabric of ruby-red, the prettiest shade of red she had ever seen.

"This is for you, Stella." Ariana placed the gift in Stella's hands. The material was so soft and floaty, yet it felt warm.

Hands trembling, Stella moved over to the window. It was a red cape!

"Oh, Mum!" Her voice quavered.

" Ace!"

"Try it on!"

Stella put on the cape and twirled three times. She loved the way it swooshed and fanned out when she moved.

"You look great," said Billy. "Just like an Alaskan Wonder-Woman!"

Ariana chuckled.

"Watch out, Princess Leia's coming!"

Stella's eyes lit up.

"Now for your present, Billy!" Ariana gushed.

She handed him the carved wand that Tom had made for him.

Years seemed to fall from Billy's face, and now he was nine years old again, playing combat games in his mom's living room.

He swished the wand in the air about his head. He loved the carving of the raven.

"Careful!" whispered Stella in Billy's ear. She knew there was something unusual about the wand. "Remember, the wood comes from Grannie-Can-Do's yard!"

The two children exchanged a glance of mock-horror that made them look like two terrible twins.

Now, even Ariana, who was usually serious, was laughing.

"Only Mom knows about that wand," she was thinking.

Stella and Billy put the red cape and the wand with their belongings in their bedrooms.

"We have an early start in the morning," said Stella, kissing her Mom "Goodnight!"

And Billy hugged his mom the biggest bear hug ever.

"Goodnight, Mom," he whispered.

"Sweet Dreams, both of you," Ariana softly said.

The flame of the candle in the living room fanned up like the wings of a bird.

And Black-Claw The Raven flew across the room to his favourite perch.

He watched the creatures of the night moving across the snow that sparkled. Then, he rested his head under his wings, dreaming of freedom and vast Alaskan skies.

CHAPTER EIGHT

Black-Claw

"Follow me!" crowed Raven, hovering over Ariana's yard. What a pretty picture they made, Stella standing there in her scarlet cape, and Black-Claw, his jet black wings in the snowy breeze!

"Get going, then!" he cawed, flapping his wings.

Stella gazed at the snow dreamily.

"Come on, Sis!" Billy said, nodding towards the sleds. They untethered them.

The dogs poured out of the cabin doorway.

Soon, they were ready.

Ariana waved from the window as the sleds glided down the slope in the direction of the alpine wood. So vast was this wood, that day became twilight, in an instant. But the comforting aroma of spruce reminded the children of Christmas.

Little winding pathways, some seldom trodden, made navigation difficult.

But with each outing, each one bringing a new challenge, Billy and Stella had learned their dogs' capabilities.

"What a pretty picture they made, Stella standing there in her scarlet cape, and Black-Claw, his jet black wings in the snowy breeze!"

Stella had made Mika, her smallest dog, the lead. She was vocal and she led the pack through barks and yelps. Moreover, she was intelligent and independent, if a little too feisty at times. She was the youngest, but who could say the young couldn't lead? Not Stella! She liked Mika's energy and spirit.

Yurairia, a swing dog, was the lightest on her feet. Stella chose her for her suppleness. She was Mika's mother. Desna, also a swing dog, was intelligent and followed the turns of the lead dog well.

Kinguyakkii, a team dog, was cheerful and spirited. Suka was the fastest and she ran in the middle, too. Stella had hopes for Suka; she had potential.

Akiak, known for her bravery and muscle, was a respected wheel dog. The dogs felt safe with her in Stella's team. Loyal Tanana, who loved the mountains, was also a wheel dog. She was the wildest of them all! Stella knew she had plenty of stamina!

Stella hoped to be higher in the rankings in this race, nearer to where she was born. The dogs deserved it! But she didn't dare say; it might jinx her luck!

How Billy missed Little Bear Dog—Miska. She was the one that was always determined. For such a small dog, she was strong. Billy hoped she was doing well. Eva would nurse her to good health again with one of her herbal remedies. To lose the leader just before the race was a cruel blow.

Eva had mentioned that Tom had a champion sled-dog, Sesi, or "Snow"—a substitute lead dog for Billy's race team. Now, Billy's heart was full of hope. If he had her, it would be some consolation. The rest of the team were all in place. Only one dog was a worry.

Eska, the first of a pair of Billy's swing dogs, was at her happiest near to water. Juneau, the second swing dog who was bred in Alaska's capital, loved the freedom of wild, open country. They were both intelligent, and worked well as a pair.

Siqiniq named after the sun, loved sunrise, and ran best in the morning. Billy knew a team always needed a good start to keep their spirits up, This dog was paired with Pakak; they were both team dogs. However, Billy had worries for Pakak; he was into everything. Whenever he sensed the mark of a bear or smelt the scent of a wolf, he went on a separate course from the pack. Billy kept him in check. He made him run in the middle to gain more experience.

Nanuq was the whitest and stockiest dog, named after the polar bear. He loved the twilight. He was a reliable wheel dog, and ran directly in front of the sled.

Ulva, the strong wheel dog with piercing eyes and a wolf-like face also favoured the semi-darkness. She was the dog that slept with one eye open, and one half-closed. Before Eva and Ariana had rescued her, and given her to Billy, she had spent her life outside. She had protected her owner from bears that prowled the yard at night and stole fish from the smoking shed.

One year, Ulva's previous owner woke to find there was not a single fish to be had. That night, Ulva had slept too well. The owner gave up on her. But now Ulva rewarded her rescuers over and over. Sometimes in that dog Billy saw himself. They were both adopted. They were both the youngest in their family, but had wisdom beyond their years.

He told his musher friends, "For me, she'd run her heart out!"

Now today, as his team raced along, Billy's voice was full of tenderness and gratitude.

"That's it, Ulva! Good Girl!"

For a few seconds, the faithful wheel dog, ears alert, looked round. They had a bond between them that was rare. She understood every word.

Brother and sister journeyed on, deeper and deeper into the forest where they planned to build a fire. When they were competing, a camp fire and a musher gathering was an invitation to talk about their hobbies and their dogs, and sometimes to tell anecdotes or stories. But today, a story unfolded before their eyes. I'm sure you've read it in fairy tales before, *"The Tale of The Raven."*

Once Upon a Time, Billy and Stella came to a clearing. Magical shafts of light penetrated the forest floor. They shaded their eyes, it seemed so bright, yet so welcoming. The rainbow lights, which reminded them of Christmas trees, danced around their feet.

"Let's stop here!" Stella called.

"You got the flasks, Stella?"

"Yes, and the sandwiches!"

Under the shade of an old spruce tree, Billy noticed the remains of a camp fire.

As the children tethered their sleds, the raven, Black-Claw, descended from the skies above them.

Only Black-Claw knew who, days earlier, had pitched a tent and lit a fire at that very spot.

Billy had a box of matches, and while the raven gathered kindling, Tom struck a match. Six times he tried. The matchbox had one match left. So the raven waited as Billy struck the seventh match. He blew on the fire and the raven fanned the flames with his blue-black wings.

"Ha! I know what you want!" said Billy.

When the fire was lit, he passed the raven some cool water in a bottle. But the bottle was half-full; try as he might Black-Claw couldn't reach the water. So, he gathered snow in his beak, and zig-zagged back and for, back and for, until the bottle was full to the brim. Then, he rolled the water-bottle under a shaft of sunlight, and waited till the ice-crystals melted. At last he had water!

Billy and Stella were amazed! They had never seen such a thing before!

"Did you know?" said Billy. "I've heard that ravens are highly intelligent birds."

"I heard that in an old Inuit tale," said Stella. "Maybe that's why our family crest is a raven."

Billy's eyes widened. He knew that everyone had high expectations of himself and of his sister. He held the walking stick first in one hand, then the other. The bird's eyes were half-human. He traced the outline of the carving. Perhaps it bestowed on him some kind of secret ancestral power.

As if the raven understood what Tom was thinking, it cawed loudly at him.

"Come on! We must get going!"

Billy scooped snow in his gloved hands and extinguished any embers that faintly glowed.

Billy and Stella untethered the dogs, hooked them up to the sleds, and called out in unison, "Let's Go!"

The moon silvered their pathway, but all around them, it was very dark and creepy.

Weird masks peered out from the tree-trunks. Silhouetted leaves made wild animal shapes that ambushed them.

"Crash!"

"Yikes!"

"Oh No!"

Stella toppled from the sled in a deep trough of snow.

"Eurgh! Billy!"

"Whoa!"

Billy jumped. Tethered his sled. Stella's dogs continued to move. The sled dug deeper and deeper into the ground.

"Whoa!" Stella called.

Billy went over.

"Hey, Sis," he whispered, gazing into her eyes.

She was not hurt. It was just the shock.

"I'm O.K, Billy."

Billy tethered her sled.

Black-Claw circled the path, descended like a dart to the spot.

Billy mustered all his strength to dig the sled out. A wide tree-trunk stump obstructed the path. What to do now? The path was too narrow, the wood around them too dense to take an alternative route.

Black-Claw flew to a nearby pine. He broke off a branch. It made a ramp.

"You sure you're O.K, Sis?" Stella lay in the snow, a Beauty from an Alaskan fairy tale.

Billy felt her pulse. Stroked her forehead. Gave her his arm.

Stella clutched his sleeve. Billy pulled her up. Now she was ready!

He scraped the snow round the sides of her sled. He released her tether.

Then, together, Billy and The Beauty, who had a feminine strength of her own, heaved and pushed, while the dogs heaved and pulled.

At last, the sled took to the air, and in one movement, shifted forwards. It rolled over Black-Claw's ramp.

"Whoa!" Stella shouted.

Billy ran ahead, released his tether.

"Hike!"

"Let's Go!"

Cautiously, they continued still deeper into the darkness.

The canopy dripped snow-melt onto them. Stella shivered.

The sleds were silhouettes, the dogs liquid shadows.

"Listen, what was that?"

A howl penetrated the silence. Something—some animal—was on their path.

More howls, in a chorus . . .

Black-Claw had a plan. As if by magic, he gave Billy the idea. Billy knew that animals had a wisdom of their own.

"Let's have the dogs pull the sleds themselves. They can return to Mom's house, away from any danger," Billy said. His voice faltered.

"I'm too tired to walk," said Stella. She stood quite still, gazed into the gloomy canopy above them.

"You don't have to!" crowed Raven.

On blue-black wings the children were lifted, soaring high above the canopy into Alaskan skies. How magnificent and mysterious the forest was! How wondrous was the sea of stars!

Below them the dogs danced among the pines, making light of the sleds and the maze. They retraced their steps, heading for the little cabin. When they reached the ramp, Sesi and Mika tipped it the other way.

As for Billy and Stella, they soared on the wings of the raven. The twinkling stars and the orbs played an ethereal, planetary music.

They need not have feared the wolves. These wolves were friendly wolves. They were Eva's forest neighbours. Long ago, Eva had rescued an orphan wolf cub and hand-fed her with her lap dogs.

And if you know anything about wolves, you know they always recognise a friend from a foe. A friend of a friend is always a friend. And a friend of an enemy is always an enemy.

Several days and nights, Black Claw sailed the skies above the canopy.

Each evening, the night swallowed the sun, and gave the raven the sun's energy. He stored this power in his black wings, tinged with the blue of Alaskan skies. Flying hundreds of miles was nothing to him.

Black Claw's wings were wide and made a comfortable bed for these dreamers who were flying.

When they emerged from over the forest, the bird headed above a little town known as Talkeetna. They followed the winding river, and flew above a railroad. Then, they turned on the wind. It guided their journey, sending them in a south-easterly direction.

Suddenly, Billy and Stella saw a magnifient ice-sculpture. The raven swooped in closer. In front of them was a shimmering rainbow, an ice tunnel, suspended above smooth, steel-gray rocks and the snow-tipped greenery below.

All at once, a beam of sunlight tinged the raven's wings blue as the summer skies. Rainbows poured from the tunnel in all directions. It was an entrance to another world.

Black-Claw flew in, set the children down to see this natural wonder. They were enveloped in rainbows. They travelled along the tunnel to the other side, behind their guide who floated on the frosty breeze.

Morning sun sent tendrils of light which played across their eyelids. Gently, softly, they awoke.

"They travelled along the tunnel to the other side, behind their guide who floated on the frosty breeze."

CHAPTER NINE

Anchorage

And so they travelled to Anchorage. It was here that Billy and Stella awoke, in a hotel in the downtown area, not far from the theatre.

Hours before, Black-Claw had bid them, "Farewell," for he was going back the same way they had come.

The raven returned through the rainbow tunnel. On the other side of the rainbow-ice, the night drank the sun, giving him renewed energy for the next day's journey. Under an ink-black sky, the bird rested, lulled to sleep by familiar sounds: the cry of friendly wolves, the sounds of moose and bears crossing the landscape—the call of the wild. Then, at sunrise, Black-Claw soared, far above the snowy peaks and the old train line, along the river, above the canopy of the wood, and headed for Ariana's cabin.

"I wonder where Black-Claw is now," Billy said to himself as he locked the door.

It was a few hours since Raven had gone.

"I think Black-Claw's reached the waterfall," Stella said. It was as if, at that very moment, she had read Billy's thoughts.

The two travellers handed in their keys.

"Have a great day!" the hotel receptionist called after them as she tidied the brochures.

Billy and Stella went through the glass swivel doors.

A shaft of sunlight played across the snow-covered path. They made their way to the little cafe at the end of the street.

"Hey, Look!" shouted Billy, squinting into the distance. "That's him! And there's Sesi!"

A tall man, with a grey-white dog on a leash was standing outside the cafe.

Billy ran ahead to meet him, and they embraced. Sesi jumped up at Billy, and Billy patted her.

Stella caught up, slip-slided her way in snow-shoes.

"Hi, Sis!" Tom said, giving her a hug. Sesi started barking.

Tom laughed.

"Are you hungry?"

"We're starving!" said Stella. Billy nodded.

"Well, there's good food in here!" Tom said, pushing the door open.

Stella found a cosy table in the corner and they all sat down. A waiter in jeans and a casual sweater took their order. He came back quickly.

Tom leaned back in his chair and smiled at him. The cafe was packed with tourists and locals, side by side. It was no easy task keeping the tables clean and attending to all the customers. It seemed as if the whole world had arrived at Anchorage!

"Good journey?" Tom said, tucking into his eggs and toast.

Billy guzzled his hot chocolate with whipped cream, nudging Stella with the end of his shoe under the table. It was code for "Don't say anything about Raven," but Tom was in on the secret; he already knew.

"Black-Claw's incredible!" he said, flashing his eyebrows. They knew that the magic was safe. They both nodded.

"Thanks for the rainbow catchers," Stella remembered.

"They catch good dreams," said Tom.

"Thanks for carving the stick. Sesi will have a good home with me, I promise."

"She's a champion racer," said Tom, buttering another slice of toast, "and won't let you down, of that, I'm certain!"

"Brilliant!" said Billy, fussing Sesi, who understood they were talking about her.

After brunch, Tom led them up the frozen path. It led to the art shop where he knew the owner.

When they arrived, he was shovelling snow from the entry. He threw down his spade.

"Well, if it isn't Tom, Ha! Ha! Good to see you!" The stocky man led the way.

Tom shouldered his way sideways through the narrow doorway, while Billy, Sesi and Stella followed.

Mac, the owner, drew up chairs near the area which stocked native carvings of every kind—hiking sticks, masks, carved picture frames, wooden signs with local names, family crests, key-chain tags and trinket boxes.

Nearby was a counter with a round bell, where customers rang for attention, and his assistant, Cory, served customers when Mac was buying in the stock.

"So what have you got for me this time, eh?" said Mac, in his straightforward manner.

Tom took out a carved statue of a bear, and another of a moose. Carved animal figurines were always popular with the tourists.

A customer who was walking around expressed an interest in the bear statue.

"Ah! It's a sample. But if you want to order one, it'll be available in two or three days."

What a stroke of luck for Tom! The customer was a school leader and their soccer team was named The Bears!

"Stella found a cosy table in the corner and they all sat down."

The customer filled in a carbon copy order form, and paid a deposit to Mac.

"Keep up the good work. An' if you can do a wall-hanging with my family crest, that'll be just great!"

Tom nodded, and shook his hand. Mac got up from his wooden chair, and walked his customer out onto the snowy pathway. When he returned, his white eyebrows and wiry gray hair were almost frozen solid. Bad weather was coming in.

"Oh heck! There's a snow storm brewing out there!" he said, stamping his feet on the coir matting. "You ready for the big race, eh?" His eyes grew round.

"Sure," said Billy with a swagger. But Stella looked less sure.

"I'm a Rookie!" she said.

Tom rubbed his chin.

"That's an advantage!" he said.

"Why?"

"No-one knows how good you are, yet!"

"I do!" said Billy. "She's good, for a girl!"

"Aw! Billy!" said Stella, pouting. "Wish I could say the same for you!"

"Good for a boy, you mean!"

"Yeah, exactly!"

Billy pulled a face back, and Stella answered. Their faces were mirror images. The terrible twosome again!

Tom laughed and told them their faces would stay like that if the wind changed direction . . .

"Now, a bit of advice for both you mushers!" said Mac, who had raced in The Iditarod when he was younger.

"It's all about the partnership between you and your dogs. Get that right, and you're in with a chance."

Billy nodded. His mind flew to his Little Bear dog. Then, he stroked Sesi's ears.

"She's a good one, Sesi is!" Tom reassured.

The dog scurried around her former owner's ankles.

Mac waved them, "Goodbye," and watched as Tom, Stella, Billy and his new dog, Sesi, zigzagged down the path, which shone like a mirror.

By the time they reached the hotel, snow came down obliquely, the sharp wind whistling round the street corners.

In the main road, traffic was bumper to bumper, cars crawling. Fog lights glared moving towards the blurry traffic lights.

When they reached the hotel, with an iron "Welcome" sign on a chain that creaked on its hinges, everyone parted their ways. Billy and Stella entered. Tom continued down the road with Sesi. He had lodgings with a family friend from the old days.

CHAPTER TEN

The Return of Black-Claw

When the raven returned from his epic journey it was mid morning. The sled dogs had emerged from their straw beds where they had spent the night after their adventure.

Ariana heard excited yelps and barks. She wondered why there was such a commotion! Then, moments later, came the answer. Black-Claw was back.

"Well here you are!" Ariana said, steepling her hands.

Black-Claw tilted his head and waited for the window to open. In he flew, taking his perch on the window-sill.

Ariana was glad to have him back. She reached into the pantry, grabbed some preserved berries, and gave the bird his reward.

Marie and Jim, Billy and Stella's cousins, were visiting. They planned to continue the dogs' training before the race. Jim was an expert musher, and dog handler. He had won two races in succession in previous years. Marie was an experienced dog handler. Her brother, her dad and his friends all planned to help Billy and Stella at the start of the race. In a few day's time, the dogs were being flown to Anchorage to get ready for the big event.

"I wonder what Billy and Stella are doing now?" Marie said.

"Tom told me he has a dog for Billy."

At this point, Little Bear, who was resting indoors with her injured leg looked up. She knew her owner's name.

Marie went over and patted her.

"I've heard Sesi's a good dog, especially when the snow's soft and powdery," Jim said.

"Yep, the snow doesn't settle like it used to. Seems to be a bit warmer than it was last year."

"What concerns me is the bit by the river. Could be the worst bit if the ice is thin and starts to melt."

"Yeah, but they did get a lot of practice!"

"Well, I think we should take 'em out again today—just on a short run before the race," said Jim.

Ariana came in from the kitchen.

"Which way are you going?"

"Not the wood."

"We're just takin' 'em on a short run," said Jim. "Then, I'll call Billy and tell him how they're all doing."

Marie and Jim donned their warm hooded coats, boots and gloves, and went outside to the dog yard.

Together, they harnessed the dogs, and checked all their equipment. Even on a short journey, things could go wrong. They were well prepared.

As they stepped onto their sleds, a shaft of sunlight illuminated the way before them.

Ariana stood in the doorway. She smiled and waved. As she exhaled, her breath made smoky patterns in the crisp air.

Raven watched at the window. And the sleds rolled down the snowy hill into the glimmer of morning sun.

CHAPTER ELEVEN

A Bird's Eye View

As the sun rose over the snowy landscape, a bald eagle warmed his wings in the mild sunlight. It soared, high above the mountain ranges, woods and rivers, high above the glaciers and peaks. The wilderness seemed untouched by man.

As Marie and Jim were speeding along the snowy trail, Jack Chapman got into his light aircraft. In minutes, he had a bird's eye view of the journey his children would soon encounter in the race of their lives.

Higher and higher the plane climbed, above the clouds that seemed to him like a rainbow carpet. Sometimes, he had the feeling he could just step out and walk the skies, gazing down on the beauty of his homeland below him. Yes! That was the thrill of flying!

From the aircraft, Jack saw caribou running along the river, moose crossing highways, people racing across the snow in their snowmobiles. He went beyond the race finish, and looped round to head for his destination.

Jack flew miles and miles, until he reached the place where tundra meets ocean. Polar bears were dancing on the ice. Still further, he flew. And in the distance, the tall cityscape that was Anchorage encroached on the wide skies. It was a giant walking an uninhabited, unclaimed land. He glanced at the controls.

"Polar bears were dancing on the ice."

Altitude—check!

Approach—check!

Prepare for landing—check!

In his mind's eye, Jack thought about the dangers that lay ahead for his children. A moose or a snowmobile approaching them during the race could take away their chances and it worried him.

So, as if taking to the skies gave him some God-like power over whatever

Fate may have in store for them, Jack planned to be there for them, watching everything!

This morning's sortie was Jack's way of taking in the most difficult part of the race—start to finish. Then, when he met them in Anchorage, he'd give them one of his pep talks to get their spirits up.

He had always been a good father, if it were not for the frequent absences his job demanded. The airline business had changed a great deal since when he was very young and a newcomer. The dangers were greater, the demands of the job meant that family couldn't always come first. He smiled to himself when he thought of the woman whom he'd married. Ariana was so practical. But unlike him, her imagination was legendary! He liked the facts. She enjoyed uncertainty. He liked control. She tossed her cares to the breeze and believed in Fate.

CHAPTER TWELVE

News From Afar!

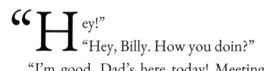"ey!"

"Hey, Billy. How you doin?"

"I'm good. Dad's here today! Meeting him tomorrow! How's everythin' goin?"

"You got good dogs! Can't believe how strong Stella's little Mika is! Your Pakak has a mind of his own. Best to keep him in the middle with Siqniq. Stella's Suka's fast! Unbelieveable! She's a good puller. We think she's a good team dog! Now, your Eska. where the ice's meltin' she's good. Junea's intelligent—a good swing dog! Ulva, now she's the one with good instincts. I know what you mean about running her heart out for ya! Strong, too! Especially for a rescue dog. Akiak's the best dog ever! Makes a good wheel dog! The shoulders on that dog, Billy! Wow!"

"Ha, Ha, yep! She's a tough one. Stella's lucky. They all ready? Tell me what you think, Jim!"

"Yeah, they're all ready as they can be."

"Great! Take 'em out tomorrow, will ya. Then, you can check 'em all in for the flight!"

"Will do! Your dad's arrived, then?"

"Yeah, um, half-an-hour ago! He has some supplies and stuff. Won't be seeing him till the mornin'—he's staying over at a friend's place."

"You gonna use the new sleds?"

"Yeah! That's the plan! Dad dropped them off before at Knik! You guys gonna be at Willow, too?"

"Sure! Your mom said she'd be there. Your gran's up for it, an' all!"

"Yep, at the start."

"Ah! She told us she'd be at the checkpoint!"

"Which one?"

"Both of them!"

"Impossible. Just like her thinkin' she can be at two places at the same time! Unless Jack . . ."

"Yeah. He'll fly her, I guess."

"Thanks for everythin', Jim. Couldn't do it without you. Stella says Hi!"

"Oh Yeah! Say Hi to Stella. Thanks!"

"You're welcome!"

"Thanks!"

"Bye."

"Later."

Billy clicked off his mobile, and glanced across at Stella who was checking them in at the hotel reception.

Jack and Tom, meanwhile, were tucking into a delicious meal of wild salmon, rice and vegetables at Charlie and Lottie Johnson's home.

"Teaching going well?" Tom said. Charlie took off his black-rimmed reading glasses, swinging them from one arm and looking directly at the speaker.

"Good year, this year," he said. "New classrooms. bigger classes, but good mix of students! A few mushers in my class like Stella and Billy!"

"Sesi, who was near the table, waited for her scraps."

"Amazing how they fit it all in," said Tom, "not like when Adrian and I were at school, eh!"

"Adrian told us you couldn't wait to get outdoors! And when that bell rang, Tom, he knew you were halfway to the gates . . . !

Tom laughed. He missed Adrian. He had emigrated to Scotland to work on a rig.

Although Jack hadn't seen his son Tom for several months, they caught up. Jack secretly admired him. As fathers and sons went, they were opposites. Tom had never left Alaska. Jack had travelled all round the world. Jack wished he could be in his native land forever, and never have to leave the place his heart loved most.

"So, you're gonna cheer them on, Dad!" Tom said with quiet determination.

"Sure!" Jack beamed.

"Want to come along for the ride?"

" Er, too much to do, Dad. We'll see, eh. I'll try."

"Ah, well," Jack said, scooping up the last few grains of brown rice with his fork.

Lottie stirred in her chair, and offered him more wine. He nodded.

Sesi, who was near the table, waited for her scraps.

Tom patted her on the head. She craned her neck. Her wet black nose twitched. Tom slung her a piece of salmon. "O.K, Buddy. Here you go!"

"Snap!"

When she'd gobbled the scrap, she circled round his legs.

Jack got up from the table, filled Sesi's water bowl, and put it down on the floor.

"There you go!" he said in his low, bright voice. Sesi's piercing blue eyes stared out from her black-gray and white coat as she nuzzled his hand.

"The dark Alaskan sky's beginning to descend, all around," Tom was thinking.

*"A single star came into view. It seemed to brighten. The light
swam across the sky like a lamp on a fishing boat at twilight."*

In his mind's eye, images of dogs flickered, their sinuous bodies a black undulating line weaving through the untamed wilderness.

At the moment, Sesi, who had finished her meal, sniffed Tom's ankles, curled up in a ball and dozed at his feet.

Tom reawakened to the moment. He made his excuses, shifted carefully from the table, and lifted the wooden window blind.

Outside, soft snow was falling, carried on a gentle breeze. It fell quietly, dusting the pathway. The instant it made earth, it seemed to melt.

He stood in silence for a moment. Then, he motioned to Jack, who joined him.

Lottie and Charlie were clearing away the dishes in the galley kitchen.

Jack nodded at Tom.

"Looks like it could be a Slush, not a Mush," he said, his brow furrowing.

"That's what I was thinking," Tom whispered back.

Meanwhile at the hotel, around 11p.m, Billy and Stella had eaten a dinner of herring in mustard sauce with fresh green salad. They retired to their rooms.

Billy gazed up at the sky which was almost opaque now.

Stella opened her window, took in the chilly night air.

A single star came into view. It seemed to brighten. The light swam across the sky like a lamp on a fishing boat at twilight. She followed it with her gaze as it darted across the sky. Then, it plummeted to the earth.

She was thinking about the race ahead. She had secret wishes, unspoken. She wouldn't tell anyone.

Everywhere around was black and dazzling white.

She closed the window, and minutes later, went to bed.

Above her was the dreamcatcher that Tom had made for her. That night wild creatures visited her. They were her friends. She had a restful night's sleep.

CHAPTER THIRTEEN

Mushers, A Chocolate Waterfall, and a Rock Man

Tom woke up the following day and peered out of his bedroom window.

"Muruaneq," he thought to himself, and smiled.

His grandfather had taught him the Alaskan Inuit words for snow, so essential for survival. And the snow was important in the race; Sesi was a great runner in these conditions, he was sure of that!

Then, he thought of something else; a trip some years back to the natural waterfall north of Anchorage, and to unknown, more remote off-grid places. Ah! If only he remembered! The general direction, he recalled, had been marked by Inuksuk men. These men were stone statues which shamens believed had magical powers to guide adventurers home.

He took Billy and Stella to a local chocolate shop and factory. It had the world's largest chocolate waterfall and an Inuksuk man.

With his earnings from dreamcatchers and carvings, Tom decided to treat them to some chocolates for the race.

He was superstitious. It was a family tradition to pay the stone man in Wild Berry Park a visit before a big racing event. Billy and Stella would be sure of a good sense of direction and good luck.

Miles away as the crow flies, Grannie-Can-Do contemplated Billy and Stella's Fate. Tonight was the pre-race meeting, when the mushers would draw the numbers. How exciting! She planned to see her grandchildren at the layover and to meet them at the race's end. Secretly, in her heart, she hoped for their success!

"Now, Tag," she whispered. "You know how dark it gets. Especially in the birch forest near the finish! Your services may be needed. I will let you know, and you can run ahead!"

Tag raced round the furniture in the dining room as if he understood every word. The trouble was, he was so excitable. He crashed into a chair leg with a resounding, "Thump!"

"And when you join the race teams, Tag, p-please be careful!"

Tag stopped, and jumped into his bed.

The raven, meanwhile, was keeping Ariana company. She was sewing a patchwork wall-hanging of The Big Race, with Stella in her red cape! Black-Claw jumped down from his aerial perch on the window sill, tilted his head and cawed.

"Raven!" she whispered, stopping the treadle. "I want you to go to Eva's, er Grannie's, O.K? She may send you off again! Billy and Stella may need your help."

The bird hopped onto her shoulder, pecked her ear gently to show he was listening.

Within minutes, Ariana had got up from her chair, and flung open the front door of the cabin. The raven soared above the great expanse of white, rainbows on his wings.

An hour later, Billy and Stella were completing their tour of the chocolate factory and shop.

"Wow!" gasped Billy, nudging Stella, who stood back with her mouth open.

In front of them, was an enormous chocolate waterfall, decorated with copper kettles.

Stella imagined she was flying on raven's wings, towards the entrance of a vast crystal-tunnel. Water-droplets made icicle tinkling sounds as the sun cast pools of colors at her feet.

Billy was reminded of the same thing.

Eva, meanwhile, in her little cabin further north, stood motionless at the door, her fingers to her mouth.

Black-Claw heard a faint whistling sound.

A flash of blue-black appeared on the horizon. The bird tilted his wings into the morning sun.

The wise woman was summoning him. She was waiting. She lifted her hand to her forehead. The wrinkles round her eyes fanned out, like fish-tails. Her animal helper had arrived!

"Black-Claw, at last!"

Meanwhile, her grandchildren were meeting Inuk Man.

"Amazin!" gushed Billy as he looked up to the stone structure that towered 19ft in front of him.

"Never seen one before," said Stella, "only in books!"

She craned her neck to read the plaque that informed visitors of the significance of stone men in Alaska.

"We are the last frontier!" Jack said. "One day, I'll fly you over the hidden territory, and you'll see more! Part of our history, they are! Guides to unchartered land!"

Tom nodded.

Stella knew that no matter how far a person travelled, there would always be places that held undiscovered treasure; the secrets of people and their hearts.

Her heart belonged in the wild. It was her Dreamworld. In her mind's eye, she lifted the snow hook. She felt the dogs surge forward. Now came the pummel of flying paws that traced fresh tracks in the snow. Stella inhaled the scent of the forests, danced under Alaskan star-filled skies.

Sometimes, as she raced, she heard an orchestra playing. And the sled seemed to fly across the snow like a bow on a violin. Everything she loved was in this moment.

Billy stood in silence by the mystical statue. Jack stood by his side. He patted him on the shoulder. Billy stuck out his jaw. He stared first at the stone man that towered above him, then, into space.

When they left, it was late afternoon.

Back at the house, Charlie answered Jack's call. He made his apologies for not going. He would stay in tonight, after all. He had piles of lesson plans to do. Besides, he had a secret. His loyalties were divided.

The others travelled a short distance to where the snowmobiles were stored.

Jack, Tom, Billy, Lottie and Stella loaded them. Then, they headed for the community center. It was 5 p.m. The pre-race meeting was about to begin.

CHAPTER FOURTEEN

All Ready for The Big Race!

Jack marched across into the community center, with Tom and the others close behind. Stella clutched her notebook tightly. Billy whistled, drove his feet deep into the snow. Jack understood. It was how he'd felt before gaining his pilot's wings.

Tom kept a close eye on them. The mushers all sat in the front row. The organisers were close to them.

"How serious they all look!" Stella thought.

But she need not have worried.

"Welcome!" a woman with a smiling face said. "Well, the good news is it's not going to be a Slush! With more new snow tonight, we're expecting soft ground, and not too much ice!"

Stella was in her gaze.

"Perhaps she knows I'm new!"

"I'm going to pass round a list of the agenda for tonight," the woman with the pepper and salt hair continued, "so please bear with me!"

There was a soft murmur from the gathering as a young lad, 12 years of age, joined the speaker giving out the handouts.

Stella was at the end of the line. She passed handouts to her left. Her handout fluttered in her fingers.

The next speaker was Mr. Walter, who informed everyone about the orange markers that lined the trail, and how to interpret the stakes along the route.

"Any questions?" he said, hands in pockets, panning the audience. One musher, a lad with sandy light brown hair from Canada, who now lived in Anchorage, had a query.

"Does anyone have any tips for a race strategy?" he said with a laugh in his voice.

Some of his friends grinned back, until Mrs. Jackson interrupted with, "Now you know we can't talk about race strategy, Nigel, that's against the rules!"

He nodded in agreement. "Just testing!" he said under his breath, glancing at his neighbor, Douglas Bywater, who looked down at the timber floor to avoid his gaze.

It was not that Nigel was a bad person. Not at all! But he was always looking for the loophole. He whispered something across to Colin. But Colin kept his eyes straight ahead.

"Right er, everyone!" Mrs. Maddox, the secretary said, clearing her throat. She peered over her glasses, which hung from a silver chain around her neck. Her hawk-eyed gaze went to the left hand side of the room where Douglas and Nigel were sitting. They sat up extra straight. Perhaps it was her titian hair that gave her an edge of authority.

"Now, Mr. Headingly will talk about the use of the G. P. S. system."

A tall stocky man with clear blue eyes strode to the front of the room.

"O.K, Folks," Mr. Headingly said in a loud whisper. When he spoke his voice made a whistling, hissing noise through his badly-fitted dentures.

"Here are some pointers for you regarding the G.P.S. We are so lucky that we have this technology on board! When I was a musher in the old days, it was old-fashioned fingers to the wind and compasses, but not anymore!"

Billy's eyes glazed over. He trusted his own instincts. They had not failed him yet. He understood that all this information was for the newbies. He looked across at Stella. She was writing down instructions. Bless her! When she was concentrating, she pointed her tongue out. She always got teased for that!

Mr. Headingly did a quick recap.

"Questions, please?"

Stella waved her hand.

"Yes, er, the girl with the reddish hair?"

"Can you just go over that bit about what to do if the G.P.S doesn't work?"

Mr. Headingly summarised the main points and with a raise of his wiry gray eyebrows he said, "All clear now?"

"Um, yeah, I think so."

Tom passed her a note, "Will explain later," and Stella gave him a faint smile.

Jack scribbled in shorthand on a notepad.

They were all looking out for Billy and Stella.

Billy, however, was unconcerned. In his heart, he felt confident. Always the sportsman, he excelled at skiing and ice-fishing in the winter, and water-sports in the summer. His sister was an expert cross-country runner. That would help. They both had good dogs. He had new hope in Sesi. No thought of failure, not a single moment of self-doubt, ever crossed his mind.

The next speaker was Mrs. Lilian White, a retired nurse, who described the emergency signal, and how to help fellow mushers in distress.

"O.K. I want everyone to practice round the room!" she said. She gave out role cards and the mushers paired up with the person next to them. Except Douglas, Nigel and Colin made a three because in total there were eleven.

Nigel tried to create a diversion, but he was outnumbered.

When the roleplay activity was over, the woman with the titian hair reappeared from the back of the room, followed by a group of girls and boys carrying gift bags.

One of the girls, Emily, spoke, while Mrs. Maddox looked on.

"We're handing out goodie bags, everyone!" she sang.

There was a short round of applause which drowned out the next thing she said.

"In these bags there are all kinds of practical things to help you. Good Luck, Everyone! Mrs. Maddox and The Junior Iditarod Commitee would like to thank all the sponsors this year for their generosity and for making this worthwhile event possible!"

Mrs. Maddox beamed, hands clasped in front of her. She stood quite still. The seasoned junior mushers knew that this was her signal for a round of applause. Clapping began with them, and slowly the others joined in. Nigel continued clapping when everyone else had finished. He slow-clapped. People stared. He stopped clapping. Then, when the others were not looking, he caught Billy in his gaze.

Billy cringed. However, the smell of cheese cooking cheered his spirits. Some men and women emerged from the kitchen; they were setting pizza down on wooden tables.

Mrs. Maddox gestured with her hands.

"Now, who would like some pizza and soda?"

People started talking all at once. She clapped.

"All right, Mushers first, then everyone, please make your way to the table!"

Stella hestitated, taking her place towards the end of the line. She hid behind her curtain of red hair. She only looked up to get her cup of soda, pizza and paper plate. Mrs. Maddox noticed, and gave her a secret wink.

CHAPTER FIFTEEN

Race Day!

Stella cut a tiny figure on the snow, wrapped up in her red cape against the elements. In her head, she heard a great orchestra tuning up. Everyone was ready! Every color of the rainbow dotted the stark winter landscape. The bleak wilderness was populated with crowds. The race flag buffeted in the wind. At intervals, orange-tipped markers signalled the long trail ahead. Visibility was good—a clear day.

The dogs were super-excited, letting out little yaps in a dog chorus! The sun cast a faint glow. The dogs made a pretty postcard picture with the majestic mountains in the distance.

Billy and Stella walked them, one by one, over the snow, paws above the ground so the dogs couldn't pull them over. Marie and Jim, their loyal cousins, who were dog handlers, and their family members, helped them get the dogs and sleds ready.

Jack beamed from ear to ear.

"Reach for the stars! You both have what it takes!"

Lottie patted Stella's arm and said, "Remember, taking part's what counts!" She nodded and smiled at Billy and said, "Good Luck!"

Now, Marie whispered something in Stella's ear. Stella half-smiled and kissed her on the cheek.

Jim and Billy stood, heads together. They were chatting about the snow, the dogs, the weather, and the trail.

Then, the signalman waved his arm, a sign that the countdown had commenced. Jack checked his watch. Ten minutes to go!

Billy and Stella tested their brakes last minute.

Everyone scattered, merging with onlookers stood behind orange netting.

Each musher took their positions.

Stella and Billy's friends were there as promised, whistling and waving their scarfs in the teams' colors.

"Hey Billy!" "Hey Stella!" "Go Billy!" "Go, Team Stella!"

Then, the man signalled the first team, and the only sound was the cacophony of dog yelps, dog howls and barks.

Billy clenched his hands in his gloves.

"Hey Sesi! Hike!"

Billy, number two musher was off!

The dogs sprang forward. Their yelps were answered by the dogs waiting for their turn.

Jack, Tom, and Lottie huddled together, looking on. Tom gazed dreamily over the tops of the trees into the distance, Lottie stood her hands in her pockets. Jack stood stamping his feet. His breath made frosty clouds as it mingled with the crisp air.

Sesi stumbled as she surged forward, but regained her footing to the cheer of the crowd. Billy adjusted the position of his sled. Now, all the dogs were mushing in unison. Stella cheered her brother on.

"That's it, That's it! Go Boy!" Jack shouted, spinning on his heels to follow the progress of Billy's sled. The sled swang round and slipped into the tree-fringed path.

"Come on, Billy, Come on, Billy! Give it some!" shouted his friends.

*"The dogs made a pretty postcard picture with
the majestic mountains in the distance."*

One of them, Adrian, who had flown in from Scotland to see the race, had just arrived at the last minute. What a surprise! He stood next to Jack whistling and jumping. The wind buffeted his blue tartan scarf.

Billy and Stella's mushing instructors stood close to the start. They didn't want to miss anything!

The press came last minute. They wanted one thing only: that elusive photograph of two contenders. One of the photographers, a short balding man from "The Anchorage Herald" adjusted the focus on his Canon camera, and scurried down to his snowmobile, hidden near the woods, clicking as he ran.

More mushers made their starts. Among them was Nigel, the one who had pulled a face at Billy at the meeting the night before.

Of course, Stella had no knowledge of petty boys' rivalries. Her eye was on her goal.

Head down, her tongue out, she adjusted her lines again. She was ready. At last, her moment came. A nervousness rippled through her body.

"Let's Go!" she half-shouted. Her voice trembled.

Stella's Irish friend, Erin, waved a dog mascot. It looked just like Mika, Stella's little lead dog.

Little Mika pulled forward, leaping skywards. They were off! The dogs' sinous bodies lunged forward. Their claws gripped the chilly air, thudded through the soft ground.

"Ah! It's so peaceful!" thought Stella, at last. Now musher and dogs were in unison, one lonely body gliding across a vast sea of snow, all alone in the quiet.

Seconds later, the onlookers were dots. The backdrop of mountains against the lake that had sheltered Stella were now hills, way behind.

Minutes passed, and the huge expanse of the snow-covered lake disappeared as they entered new territory.

"Gee!"

Yuraria and and Desna, the swing dogs, curved the direction of the sled to the right. It swooshed ahead and took a narrow path through spruce trees that fringed the trail on either side.

They slowed their pace. The path, covered with newly-fallen snow, had visible trails from the teams at the front. The path through the woods curved again. Now, through the trees, a musher appeared. There he was, just minutes ahead!

In that moment, however, Stella felt alone in the wilderness, alone with her dogs. She had a vague feeling that her father would be proud of her. She held a clear conviction that if, by some miracle of fate, she were the victor, all her financial worries would be over. She planned to go for a Music major. In her free time, she practised violin. People were surprised when she told them. An outdoorsy girl, with a passion for music? Mushing and music, an unlikely combination.

But in her head, she believed what Einstein had suggested. The enigma of The Universe itself was answered in mathematics. Mushing was all about timing. It was about the rhythm of dog and man—synchronicity of movement, elegance. And sometimes, the movement of her bow across the strings of her violin reminded her of the swish and glide of the runners on a sled ride in the snow.

The copse of trees shut out the sky at intervals. Between them were gaps; snow, tinged with the faint light of the morning sun, alternated with shadows. This reminded her of all life's joys and sorrows. The trail was Life itself, unfolding. A rookie musher, sure, she had practised at mushing school. Today, she saw the trail more clearly than ever. This new vision was unexpected. She felt a strange combination of elation and nervousness.

Meanwhile, Lottie, a first time spectator at the race and an empath, was cheering her on in her head. They were on their way back to Anchorage.

"I wonder where our Stella is now!"

In her mind's eye she saw the red cape. This cape had become Stella. Bold, Bright, Daring, Red! It was a girl in a story-book. Stella was a star on the red carpet, in Hollywood. What a bright smile she had! That photograph! That trophy! And that red hair that flowed like a mane in the wind!

"This cape had become Stella. Bold, Bright, Daring, Red! It was a girl in a story-book . . . Ah! Surely it was Passion . . .

Passion that played music and danced across the snow!
Sometimes, this Passion ran with the wolves."

It was triumph and glory. But, Oh! Perhaps it was a red flag, spilt blood. Maybe it was the fight. Danger, even. Ah! surely it was passion . . . Passion that sang! Passion that painted Alaskan sunsets! Passion that played music and danced across the snow! Sometimes, this passion ran with the wolves.

She promised herself to start her painting. Ariana was doing the wall-hanging. She'd ask her, first.

"Well, a good beginning for Billy. Held that together well!" Jack enthused. "More difficult for Stella, though. Bib number 7. Yep, there's a bit of ground to cover. But I'll say one thing. That girl's got her head screwed on."

"You're going to follow 'em, Dad?"

"Yeah, I guess we'd better get going," Jack shrugged. He pointed to the area with snowmobiles. "You are coming then, Tom? No work today, eh!"

He grinned. He liked being alone. But the thought of Billy, his little brother, a true winner, and Stella, his little sis with the best of them, who'd ever have thought of that!

"Yeah! Why not?"

And with that, Tom and Jack strode together side by side. Their boots crunched and crackled in the snow as they left the crowd.

In Juneau, the capital of Alaska, Stella's best friend, Louise-Ann Du Lac, was watching the race on live G.P.S satallite, "Race Insider." As Stella's sled curved into the little copse of trees she sprang out of her seat, and pirouetted across the living room. She was a musher dancer. Older than Stella by a year, a month later, she was entering The Iditarod—Anchorage to Nome.

Stella promised that if she came in the first three, the two friends would compete with one another in a year or two.

In the crowd, further on, some of Stella and Billy's non-mushing friends had gathered.

"Great about Billy," Alan gushed.

Stella did not know. But further down the trail, Billy, who was number 2, and the race favorite, had set a good pace.

Sesi had turned out well. But sometimes, Billy wondered. He had only just adopted her. He missed Little Bear Dog's tenacity, her ability to understand him. What's more, one of Sesi's paws was giving her some trouble. The checkpoint veterinary was his best hope.

He felt lonely. That was one of the problems of being the leader. Now, he imagined how Stella had felt being the elder sister, being the first born. He had learned from her mistakes. She had been Ariana's experiment. He and Stella were adopted. He was the youngest in the family, and sheltered. Now, in the race, he understood what it meant to be exposed. He was out in front, giving it his all!

CHAPTER SIXTEEN

Up, Up and Away!

Jack and Tom, meanwhile, whizzed through the powdery snow alongside the race trail for a short distance. At intervals, they saw team colors that flashed through the trees of the copse, making an up and down motion as the mushers progressed. These mushers were near the starting line.

Then, they followed the race in Jack's airplane.

"It's a good day for flyin!" Jack said as they approached the light aircraft. Their steps were in time. Every so often, Tom, who was shorter than Jack, gazed up to meet his steady gaze.

Jack's expression was calm and relaxed, but his eyes betrayed the excitement he felt for his kids. Tom walked more upright than usual.

"Well, let's hope they do us proud, eh, Tom," said Jack, taking off his cap, to shake the snow.

Tom nodded.

Jack opened the plane door, and motioned to Tom to take the front passenger seat.

Jack went through his checks. Soon, the plane was trafficking across the makeshift runway that snowploughs had cleared.

The plane lifted, and out came the wing flaps. It climbed up into grey-white Alaskan skies. There was just a hint of a glow: the beginnings of a new dawn.

Behind them, the majestic snow-capped mountain tops sparkled with cool sunlight.

Tom peered from the side window.

Below him, the mushers on the trail were now miniature action figures with toy dogs pulling the sleds. At the rear, near the start of the wooded area, they bunched together. Then, they thinned out. Tom spotted a dark-haired lad with blue colors.

"Who's that?"

Jack adjusted the altitude, the plane dipping at a safe height, just clearing the tree-tops.

"That's William!"

He was swapping his lead dog who was not on form.

"William? number 5!" I'm surprised! Way behind Billy! Didn't expect that!"

Two mushers, numbers 6 and 4, heads down, were untangling sled-lines.

The trip through the forest had been eventful.

"Hey! There's Stella!" Tom shouted, pointing out of the starboard window Stella's red cape was unmistakable. It flew like a magic carpet behind her. It dazzled against the virgin-white of the snow.

A little further on, in open country, they saw a group of caribou. Global warming meant the deer had ventured out early this year. It was as if the clock of nature had marched forward. It was almost spring!

Seconds later, Jack and Tom exchanged a glance. But neither said a word. There was the enemy, number 3, and he was gaining ground!

About a mile from the starting line was a dirt road that crossed the dogsled trail. It had frozen into ice. A sharp wind carried the snow, making steep drifts on either side.

A woman in an orange overall was standing in the middle, waving someone through.

Tom spotted him! A musher was carving a trail through wind and snow, faster than in the forest. One of the dogs had a distinctive grey-white pelt. The musher had dark hair.

"Look! Our Billy!"

"Is it?" .

There was something about the familiar dog's gait that seemed unusual.

"Eurgh!" said Tom. "Somethin's wrong with Sesi!"

"No?"

Jack tilted the plane and went in a little closer. Sure, Tom was right. He knew his dogs. But he wasn't allowed to communicate with Billy, for that was against the rules.

"He'll have to unhook Sesi and stow her on the sled." Tom muttered.

There was a silence between them. Jack paused for a moment.

"He'll get a checkover at Yentna."

"Yep! He sure will. Billy's one for looking after those dogs." Tom said."I told them both—Look after the dogs and they'll look after you!"

The plane hovered above the trail. Jack observed the scene unfolding.

Seconds later, Billy came to a halt. He looked over his shoulder. Nigel's shadow was not far behind him.

"Number 3, er Nigel, that's him . . . Doesn't like Billy one bit!" Tom said as an afterthought.

"Ah! Why?" Jack said. He narrowed his eyes.

"Ever since he beat him at Yukon! Not a good loser. Never talks to him now. Used to be best friends!"

"Yeah," said Jack, examining his knuckles. Keeping up with all Billy's mushing friends was difficult at times. "Now, I remember. But when Billy won, he never said much about it. Didn't want to make him feel bad!"

"Yep, that's right. But Nigel's bent on winning this time. He'll still talk to Stella. He thinks she's just a girl—no threat to him, see!"

"A little further on, in open country,
they saw a group of caribou."

"He'd better not count on that!" said Jack. "May the best one win—man or woman! That's what I say! Stella works hard. Who knows what will happen?"

"Be nice if they both got rankings."

"Well, the toughest bit of the journey is yet to come," said Jack, adjusting his speed.

"What bit?"

"Billy says it's from the woods towards the end into Willow, when it's pitch black, and you're exhausted! Let's hope he makes it! But then, Stella says the most challenging's the longest part to Yentna."

"Dad, I never realised you kept up with it all!" grinned Tom.

Jack smiled with his eyes.

"Just because er, my job takes me away, er, it doesn't mean I don't think of them." He reached into his flying jacket and drew out a photograph.

"Remember, eh, Tom."

It was the group family photo. Tom was 16, Stella, 9, and Billy, 8. They were standing outside Grannie-Can-Do's cabin with their first ever sled dogs in the depths of winter. At Billy's feet, in the snow, was Little Bear Dog, and a wolf-dog, Ulva, with fire in her eyes. Stella held tiny Mika in her arms. Tom had an older dog at his feet, Sesi. The name meant, "Snow." Grannie-Can-Do, in her purple cape, stood alongside them with Black-Claw, the raven, perched on her shoulder. Ariana was the other side with Tag, the cute red fox, at her ankles. You would never know from the smiles how cold it was! Jack wasn't in the photo; he was the photographer.

"Wow, Dad," said Tom, his eyes glistening with emotion.

"Can't believe where the time has gone . . ."

Jack's eyes gazed upwards; he searched for a memory. "Remember when Grannie-Can-Do said she didn't want Stella to race?"

Tom smiled a faint smile, lifted his eyebrows. "She wouldn't say that now."

Jack understood. Ariana had told him that "G. C. D" as she was known for short was "helping" Billy and Stella in the race.

"The only thing that will get them through is skill and effort—and that means reaching for the stars! It's all in the ability of the musher and his dog. It's all about the relationship. They have to be a good team!"

Precision was Jack Chapman's middle name. "Study the trail!" he had said over and over to Billy and Stella. "Practice! Don't be soft on those working dogs. But look out for them! Every one of them is different. Know your dogs, their strengths and their weaknesses!"

The light aircraft buffeted on the air currents. Below them, now, was Fish Creek.

Still further on, they saw the place where all the trails intersected with one another. The landscape breathed like a body; the trails were veins and arteries that gave it life. This way and that snowmachines were flying; the snow churned with activity.

"Let's hope they don't get lost!" Jack said, pointing out of the window.

Tom frowned. He was thinking about Stella. Then, he spotted Seven Mile Lake. How empty is seemed, and how lonely! It reminded him of a white ocean, stretching ahead. And the mushers were sailors, charting undiscovered new horizons, fraught with danger.

Minutes later, below them loomed Nine Mile Hill.

"Look at that!"

Not one musher! It stood like a symbol of the struggle ahead.

Jack knew what Tom was thinking. It was a long, hard trail.

CHAPTER SEVENTEEN
Magic!

Back at her cabin, not far from the woods, Ariana sat at her sewing machine, making the outlines for her hanging tapestry. In her mind's eye, she saw the whole panorama. The sun, rising in the morning sky at the beginning of the trail, the snow and the little copse where the sleds swooshed up and down the serpentine paths following orange markers as they went.

At the first sign of light, she had sent Black-Claw ahead. Unseen, the bird was hidden in the branches of a spruce tree when Billy passed. Only the raven saw what happened.

"Give Trail!" Billy had shouted to Nigel, who had already overtaken him, once!

Nigel made way.

Perhaps the dogs sensed some secret unspoken rivalry.

As Billy overtook him, the path narrowed. Minutes later, Pakak, the most inquistive dog, a middle dog on Billy's team, yelped and turned his head. Sesi, the lead dog, was distracted and stumbled. She yelped, louder than the first dog. And Eska, one of the swing dogs behind her, got a little too close. The dogs lost their momentum.

"Whoa!"

Some of the dogs continued forward, while others at the front, stopped.

The sled, which was traveling downhill, trundled to a halt. The dogs piled on top of one another. It was a scrum! Billy put the dogs in position and tied the sled to a nearby tree with the snub line. He spent a few minutes untangling the line. He checked Pakak. All good. But when he lifted Sesi's back left paw, she pulled it away. He tried again, and this time, he freed her from the tangle. He had to make a decision on the spot. It was only a small cut. She was the leader. It could wait till the checkpoint. He applied some ointment, put the bootie back on, untied the snub line.

"O.K, Sesi, Hike!" he said to his team, in a warm voice of encouragement, and they started up again.

Billy checked behind him. Yards away, there he was again, breathing down his neck. Nigel, enemy number 3.

Billy signalled his dogs a secret signal that only they, Billy and Black-Claw, the secret watcher, knew. It meant, "Speed Up!" Up and down the woodland slopes they went as fast as possible. Sesi was running better now. But he heard an ominous whistle behind him.

"I can make more distance between us on the next part."

He envisioned the trail ahead of him. The first dirt track that crisscrossed the frozen trail was ahead. Then, he had eight miles to go to reach Nine Mile Hill.

As the sled left the wood, Billy glanced over his shoulder. He looked at his waterproof watch. He'd widened the gap.

At that moment, in the periphery of his vision, he noticed a flash of blue-black raven's wings. Black-Claw soared into the trees that sparkled with snow-melt, warming his wings under the mild morning sun.

Time flew. Billy fought the snow that stung his mouth and lashed at his cheekbones.

Stella cried out to her dogs to do her bidding.

So far, they hadn't let her down. They were both living their mushing dream and gaining ground . . . Yet neither one of them knew the other's fate.

Meanwhile, what home comforts had been waiting for Charlie and Lottie! As brother and sister were doing battle, they were at home, following the action on "Race Insider" while they had brunch,

"Billy!" said Lottie, clapping her hands together.

"Yep!" said Charlie. "Billy's in the lead again." His voice sounded flat. Billy had started on the approach to the zig-zag trail that took him to the mountain top.

"Look at that hill!"

"That's the killer!" said Charlie, "Nigel, d'you know him? He's in my class. He's tipped to be at the front. He told me about that! Any weak dog it'll bring out the worst in 'em, and any good dog, the best in 'em!"

Lottie gave Charlie a questioning look.

"Good luck to all of 'em," Charlie added. His boy was close behind Billy.

The camera panned in on the dogs. Billy's Sesi was pulling with all her might despite her injury.

"Long way to go yet!"

Charlie nodded. What would happen in this race was anybody's guess!

Charlie did the dishes, Lottie did the drying.

"Must call Eva. We have a lot of catching up to do!"

"Ask her if she needs a lift to Yentna!" Charlie said. "Tom's with Jack. But my old school friend, Frank, is a pilot. He's not far from Eva's. He can pick her up!"

Lottie nodded.

"Mm. Ariana," Lottie whispered out loud to herself. She decided to call her as well. She needed some advice.

"Eva!" came the voice. It was a voice that had the quality of a flute— light, bright, and airy.

"Lottie!" smiled Eva, who stood, telephone in hand, looking out of the window for the bird with the blue-black wings.

"Frank, er, you know who I mean, your neighbour, has offered to take you to Yentna, if you want. We thought you'd like to see them all coming in. His wife's one of the volunteers. And his daughter's one of the cooks at the lodge."

"Ya, that'd be just great!" said Eva.

"We'll let Frank know, then, and he can phone you."

"Thanks!"

"Keeping out of mischief?"

Eva's involvement in the race was quite natural. Any grandmother would do their best for their grandchildren. Anyway, Black-Claw and Tag were just animals. If they could give the kids a little encouragement, what was wrong with that?

"Eva? Are you there!"

Of course, um, I am, Dear," said Eva with a laugh in her voice.

"That's good!" trilled Lottie.

"Keeping busy, then?"

"Ya, a bit of this and that. Was just listening to Stella playing the violin. That recording. Christmas. She was only 9 when she played that song—Concerto in F Major—Northern Star."

"Yes! I remember that Christmas," breathed Lottie. "Stayed overnight. We were snowed in. Stella entertained us. You'd just bought the dogs! Tom was er, 17?"

"16"

"That's right. Um, er. What was I saying?"

"About the night you stayed with us!"

"Oh yeah! Well those kids have grown. 'N Tom's come out of his shell a bit. He and Jack—two peas in a pod!"

The two women reminisced about old times. Lottie took her phone to the window. Outside, the morning sun glinted through the mountain tops. And there were rainbows in the clouds.

CHAPTER EIGHTEEN

Eva Makes Plans

"Gran, I just want to take part. I know I messed up last time. But there were a lot of mushers with more experience. And the race was fast . . . I'm going now. Have to get an early night. It'll be an early start! Bye, Gran. Don't worry!"

These words echoed in Eva's mind as she poured a cup of blueberry tea and sat down by Tag, who was in his bed, dozing, although it was almost mid-morning.

"Ah! I hope that Stella's got over those nerves!"

Then, she thought of Billy. She wondered about Sesi. Although she was a good dog, she had belonged to Tom. Billy was so attached to Little Bear Dog. She was on the mend. But, too late. That could make a difference to his race. And then, of course, there was the sandy-haired boy—freckled face, gangly.

"What was his name. Dash! What was it, now?"

Eva sprang out of her chair and toppled her cup in the saucer. A pool of blueberry tea dripped from the rustic table onto the wood floor.

"Damn!"

Holding on to the cabinet, she steadied herself and lifted her ankle. Nothing was broken, not even a sprain. No more than a slight bruise.

Eva mopped up the remainder of the spilt brew, plunged the mop in the bucket in the kitchen, and returned to her tapestry armchair.

"Ya! That's him! Second, the year before last! And Billy, bless him—the winner!"

She put on her glasses with mother-of-pearl wings. Flicking to the next page of her magazine, she studied the familiar picture—the one of Billy lifting his trophy, head high, while Nigel looked on.

"Fierce competition!" Eva muttered. The kids had to learn to deal with the challenges ahead.

"I'll do what I can, when I can." thought Eva, patting the little fox.

"Now, that isn't interfering, is it, my precious!" laughed Eva, lounging back in the armchair as if she had just put the whole world, at least, her little world, Alaska, to rights.

Black-Claw had returned from his earlier outing. He hopped round on the window ledge and expanded his wings. The sun was beginning to move round. It was a little warmer than the first light of dawn in the woods.

As if she read the bird's thoughts, Eva said, "Now Raven, you and Tag are coming with me on the plane! Frank'll be here later on. And we'll arrive at Yentna early evening, in time to see the mushers come in! We must work out a plan. You both can help when you are needed!"

Black-Claw cawed and hopped onto her shoulder. He pecked her ear. This was his code for, "Understood, G. C. D! Yes, Ma'am!"

Tag stirred in his bed, his amber eyes gazing into the distance.

Frank, meanwhile, who lived two miles from Eva as the crow flies, was making preparations for the stopover at Yentna.

Lists were Frank's thing. If one made lists, then nothing was forgotten. His wife, Dorothy, known at Dottie for short, was already at Yentna. Her job was to wave the mushers in as they arrived, and keep them on the right path.

Dottie had told Frank to be sure to fly in the straw for the dogs, half a bale each team, for five teams. She also asked him to bring two sleeping bags and two pairs of thick, woolly bedsocks.

"Ah! And a flask of coffee," Frank said, screwing on the cap to the thermos. "Oh! And those chocolates donated by the chocolate shop in Anchorage." He opened the pantry doors. *"Yes!"* He opened one of the foil-wrapped chocolate coated caramels, threw up in the air, and caught it in his mouth. "Yumee!" He went into the bedroom. "And a spare stopwatch." It was in the middle draw of the chest of drawers. "Hum! And the tin-opener . . ."

Frank sprang around the cabin like someone a decade younger than his years. When he reached the bottom of the list, he checked off the last item with a flourish.

Snow was falling, lightly, softly all around.

"Stella'll like this. A slower race."

At the hanger was his pride and joy—the light aircraft he'd bought on his 50th birthday! It gleamed like brand new! He checked it over, closed the hanger doors with a grunt of satisfaction. Then, he trudged over to the front door of the house and peeled off his boots.

Frank Smith exhaled—satisfied with the morning's work, and sat down to enjoy a well-earned cup of steaming hot ground coffee in his favorite mug.

He switched on the stereo. His favorite song was playing, "My Country."

Thoughts of his love affair with the Alaskan skies, the beasts that roamed its lush forests, the meandering waterways, where he spent tranquil hours in childhood and adulthood, fishing in quiet solitude, entered his mind. He was, indeed, a lucky man.

CHAPTER NINETEEN

Coming Round The Mountain

Billy had opened up a five minute lead ahead of Nigel, when he approached Nine Mile Hill.

In the distance, the hill had looked easy, but now, yards from the base, it looked like a mighty challenge.

"Haw!" he shouted to Sesi.

But Sesi did not respond, and instead, she took the lower path, sharp right.

"What's wrong with you?" Billy snarled as the sled whipped round the low road, the team dogs flexing muscle to keep the momentum going in the biting wind.

"Whoa!" Billy shouted. But did the dogs stop? No way! That Sesi had a mind of her own.

Whether he felt the pressure of a champion when he'd asked for the left hand turn, or whether he felt the presence of Nigel's shadow looming closer, who knows?

"Sesi! Hey, Sesi!" Billy protested.

The sled continued. Then all of a sudden, a sharp "bump" of the runners as the sled swung left brought Billy to his senses.

He had missed the sign! Sesi had led the dogs herself!

"Thank God for a dog with a mind of her own," he muttered to himself.

Then he laughed, warm tears rolling down his pink cheeks. Was he going mad?

Of course not! There was a vague throb behind his eyes. Yet now, he felt lighter . . .

One lapse of concentration, one error of judgement; he had tried to send Sesi on the route they used as a practise run. He was so tired he'd switched to automatic pilot. That route to the right would have taken them close to the edge. One mistake, and you lost your life and the life of your dogs.

"Get a grip!" Billy said to himself. "We are going to make it!"

With Sesi's savvy intelligence they did make it. They did more than that! On the other side of the mountain, they were still in the lead.

So, Tom was right about Sesi:

"She'll never let you down!"

Now, Billy knew his faith in her was not misplaced.

By the time Nigel and his team were halfway round the mountainside, Billy was ready to cross the second dirt road, nine miles from the start.

Straight ahead, a figure dressed in luminous orange signalled that familiar road. Her frizzy blonde hair buffeted in the wind. It was Mrs. O' Sullivan, the first human he had seen for some time.

Sesi slowed down automatically.

Billy turned round. Nobody yet.

"Whoa!" instructed Billy. A truck was coming along the dirt road. The blonde-haired woman stood on the track, her hands raised above her head, her big stop-sign facing the truck driver who came to a gradual halt. Then, Mrs. O'Sullivan waved Billy through. The dirt road was slippery and uneven.

The shadow of Nigel in Billy's young imagination was a spectre that haunted him. Billy was determined not to let him win. Never! No Way! There was a prize at stake! But no, he didn't want to go to college. He vowed to himself that if he won, he would give some of his winnings to Stella, then she could go. Some would go to the mushing teams. Some would go to Granny-Can-Do to make her old age easier. And some he would put away, until he knew what his Destiny was. He only knew one thing. In spite of everything, he would never give up mushing. It was his life, that, and the dogs.

By the time Stella reached the hill that from a distance had looked like a mountain, she smiled a smile of reasurrance. It was a revelation—she saw that nothing was impossible.

When she was small, Ariana would read to her all the fairy tales and legends set in Alaska. They were stories of ancient Inuit tribes who crossed the sea and navigated the land, hundreds of miles across vast glaciers, lush forests, mountains, lakes and rivers.

The sea was inhabited by The Qulupaik, a half-human creature with green skin and long hair, who waited to ambush children, unawares. The Tizhenick, snake-like creatures also lived there. They snatched people from docks and piers.

In the story book, back at Grannie's house, Stella remembered the tale of the wolf who gobbled wayward daughters. He was a forest dweller. Now, Stella was young woman. Even so, these fables replayed, touching the innermost chambers of her heart.

Stella's Alaska was part of her, and she vowed, at that moment, to make it her own.

For Stella, the mountains each had their story. They were freedom. When she played her violin, the drifts of music carried her to a special place —The Sleeping Lady at Susitna—where, the story goes, snow fell softly for the very first time on this land known as Alaska. The Sleeping Lady slept under the blanket of snow. She was waiting for her lover to return. Spring came, and wild flowers peeped their heads through the snow-blanket. For Stella, these flowers represented Hope.

While she was having this little daydream, her loyal dogs kept going; they knew the route round the mountain via the lower road and further on where they would cross the little track.

All of a sudden, a vision of white came into view. On the side of the snowy mountain track, two sure-footed goats were grazing.

For a few seconds, she gazed at the majestic animals. They each had two jet black horns, and thick, white winter coats. In a vision, she saw these animals represented tenacity. They held on to the mountainside, and the mountain, far from being a challenge, sustained them.

One last glance over her shoulder. No-one in view.

"Easy!" she shouted. One of the goats watched as Stella's sled sped round the mountainside. Then, Stella Honor Chapman gave her command at the sign, swinging the sled onto Burma Road. Her yellow log at the ready, she passed through the first checkpoint.

"All of a sudden, a vision of white came into view. On the side of the snowy mountain track, two sure-footed goats were grazing."

*"One of the goats watched as Stella's
sled sped round the mountainside."*

CHAPTER TWENTY

Grannie Sets Off!

After his cup of ground coffee and ten minutes of quiet time, Frank donned his warmest blue jacket and woolly hat, and made his way over to the old hanger way back in his yard.

It was ten thirty. He planned to be at Grannie Can Do's just in time for another cup of coffee and a slice of her famous Baked Alaska Dessert!

There his pride and joy stood! On the side of the airplane was the Alaskan flag. To Frank, that flag always reminded him of the song. The one that told of starlit skies, meandering mountains, clear seas and rivers. How proud he felt! How good it was for young ones to get out among beauty and nature. It was all here, in Alaska! And in their own small way he, Frank Smith, and his wife, Dorothy Indigo Smith, were helping to make it all happen!

Grannie, meanwhile, danced around her bedroom, rummaging through her clothes from the huge closet. They made a big rainbow pile on the floor. What to wear for the race? She settled on a pair of blue jeans and a bright electric blue sweater. Stella and Billy would see her in the crowd. She put on red crystal earrings, a red scarf with a silver star brooch, and ruby red sneakers. Stella would understand she was rooting for her. After all, Billy had won the race at Yukon! It was Stella's time now.

"If only she had more confidence in herself. Those nerves. It's always the ones who are talented who have self-doubts."

Minutes later, Grannie-Can-Do stood in the middle of the room, and shouted, "Well, Stella of The Red Cape! You're going to show 'em!" But of course, no-one heard. Only Black-Claw and Tag, who both looked at her at the same time. Soon, they thought, it would be time to go.

Black-Claw flew up to the bedroom window-sill. And little Tag, sensing the excitement, did three laps of the bedroom!

"Ha! Tag! Save your energy! We're going on a big journey! When we get to Yentna Station you can run around all you want!"

Tag's amber eyes lifted to meet Eva's gaze. She reached down and stroked his soft red fur. For a moment, Tag stood still. Then, his paws began to dance on the spot. Then, he burst through the bedroom door, landing at the entrance of the cabin. There were three loud knocks.

"Eva! It's Frank!"

Eva shuffled to the door in her slippers.

"Hey Frank!" she said, embracing him.

Frank's thick black eyebrows were frosted with the snow. He banged his leather gloves together.

"Come in, and I'll make some coffee!"

"Everything ready?" smiled Eva.

"Yep, I think so," Frank said, taking the chair nearest the table. His eyes alighted on the Baked Alaska.

Eva followed his gaze.

"Now, er, Frank. How about some of my Baked Alaska?"

She took a silver serving spoon from the drawer and two dessert spoons. She reached into the cupboard and brought out two earth-brown coffee mugs and two earthenware plates.

"Well, make yourself at home!" Eva brushed the flour from her cook's apron with her hands. "So, how's our Dottie!"

At the mention of Dottie's name, Frank beamed.

"Ah! She's all geared up for the race! We got her one of 'em bright jackets—yellow it is—so it shows up when she's signalling 'em. Don't want any of them to get lost now, do we, eh?"

Eva nodded. She hoped Stella understood the new G.P.S system. She was never one for all that technology! Still, it was different to her young days. Girls! Girls racing! Who ever would have thought of that!

When Frank offered her a second helping of her own Baked Alaska, Eva chuckled.

"Have as much as you want, Frank!" Eva said, scooping him another piece.

They laughed in unison. Then, Frank went all quiet again.

The meringue melted in his mouth—it was legendary!

"All set?" Frank said, his plate clear. He rose from his chair.

"Yes, I mean, No, um, wait a minute!" Eva said, untying the apron.

She disappeared into the bedroom. Frank waited and waited. He thought he heard a voice chanting very softly. An alluring scent, like the aroma of incense, eminated from Eva's room. He heard a voice chanting again. The voice was at a distance, but came closer. A mysterious sound pierced the air. He got up, looked out of the window. The sun, that illuminated the snow-drenched treetops, highlighted a fast-moving animal. On the horizon. nose to the ground, it zig-zagged through the treeline. It was a wolf.

Eva reappeared. Nothing about her was any different as far as Frank could tell. Why did women take so long to get ready? Then he noticed. Around her neck, Eva wore a silver necklace. The pendant had a moon in silver, and a bird in flight, etched in copper, with black detail. It was a raven!

"That's a nice necklace!" Frank said.

"Oh, Thank you, Frank," Eva said, clutching the round disc on the end of the chain. "Ariana made it. It's an amulet," she said with a special emphasis. "My daughter's clever, you know!"

Frank nodded. He wondered why women were so superstitious. It seemed to him they lived in a very different kind of Universe.

"I don't know that I believe in all of that! You know people make their own kind of luck!"

For what seemed like hours, they exchanged all the stories of their lives; Eva about her equestrian days, how she met her husband, had Ariana and was widowed, and Frank about Dottie Indigo, his wife, and her work for The Iditarod Committee. He talked about Candy, their daughter, who did voluntary work, and how she wanted to be a veterinary surgeon.

"Girls have careers now!"

Eva paused and said, "Yes, they do! Well then, how about a little light lunch, Frank, before we leave?"

Frank nodded. Her cooking was alchemy! There was plenty of time for venison stew! Perhaps, after all, she would not be interested in his old stamping ground. They decided to take the shorter route.

It was mid afternoon when Eva packed her light luggage. She opened the book with the fairy tale that was lying on her pillow. What an uncanny resemblance there was between the little girl in the cape and her grand-daughter!

Frank gazed out of the kitchen window. The sun had moved round, casting long, finger-like shadows of trees across the snow.

When they had finished their meal, Eva went into her room, and busied herself with the packing.

"Ready, Gal?" Frank called, looking at his watch. He rapped softly at the door. "Thanks, Frank," Eva said as he picked up a blue holdall with red handles.

Eva stood at the bedroom door for a few minutes. Black-Claw was perched on her shoulder. She left her door half-open, took her red scarf from the brass hook in the hall, scooped up Tag, and went outside.

CHAPTER TWENTY-ONE
Stella's Progress.

The rugged terrain of the mountain trail, all the uphill climb, and the downhill slide had pushed Stella to the limits. Now, in open terrain, she felt a chill wind cut across the trail. Ahead of her was a steep bank, several feet high. Over the dogs paws flew; the sled alighted onto the lake. The vast expanse of white stretched to infinity. They stopped, and refuelled.

"Good Dog," she said, stroking little Mika, who had the lion's share of the salmon. But Stella was always fair. She talked in whispers as she fed each one. Her dogs answered her; Mika answered in little yaps and jumps, the Team Dogs in yelps that echoed one another. Tanana replied in yips and howls. The Swing Dogs, Desna and Yurairia, had glistening, sharp eyes that gazed wistfully into the distance. Akiak was the strong silent one that brushed up against Stella's legs.

"I'm here. Are we going yet?"

Sometimes, when Stella gazed deep into her eyes, she seemed half-wolf, half-human.

Stella travelled with a kind of double-vision. Her near vision was on the team of faithful dogs.

Mika was a ball of energy as usual. Yuraria seemed to dance across the ice. But out of all the dogs, Suka was at her happiest on this long but fast leg of the journey.

Stella worked the dogs, shouting instructions, coaxing them forward. Beyond the lake, the going was hard, uphill and downhill. The heat of afternoon sun slowed the dogs' pace. They were panting. She got off the sled, holding on and pushing it forward to help them.

She often looked back. Bunched together, was a group of challengers. Her long vision was always on the horizon. At intervals, ahead of her, she caught glimpses of Billy, and the sandy-haired boy from Canada.

Now, she wondered how her little brother was doing.

Just as her thoughts turned to Billy, she saw a foreboding sight. Two antlers silhouetted against the sky. One false move now, and she'd put her dogs in danger. She slowed the sled to delay her arrival. She hoped the moose would move off, that danger would pass.

"Whoa!" she called and the sled came to a halt. The moose was within striking distance. It stomped its feet. It tossed its antlers to the wind, and ran. Now, it was just visible on the horizon. Stella and her team were safe.

"Phew! Let's Go!"

She continued up the west side of a river, through the woods, and onto a partly-wooded swamp.

The Nome sign appeared at a fork in the trail. "Haw!" she shouted. The sled curved round, following the golden arrow and heading through open swamps and through the trees.

In the river's ravine, Nature was cruel. Overflow and steep turns made the going difficult. The winding path took the team downhill onto the river creek bed. Then, they climbed up the other side.

The trail led to another creek after about one mile. The hill took them to Flathorn Lake.

Snowboarders were criss-crossing the trails interwoven in all directions.

Through the trees they journeyed. Stella fed the dogs again.

The trail continued through the swamps, and big cottonwoods. It dropped down to the river.

In the snow, Stella spotted a blue glove. Had something happened to Billy?

She looked all around. Nothing. No-one. And pressed on.

Down on the river, she followed the orange markers on a kind of auto-pilot. The dogs led the sled, Stella was preoccupied. What about Billy? She hoped he was safe.

She was approaching the checkpoint, Su River, at 1.20 p.m. She arrived at 1.30, minutes behind two lead mushers.

"How many dogs?" said the man at the checkpoint. Stella produced a yellow log.

"Everything O.K?"

She left minutes later, heading towards Eagle Song.

Billy, meanwhile, had passed the checkpoint. He was blazing a trail in front of her. But Nigel, the contender, was ahead of him.

On the open road, Nigel had propelled the sled faster and faster. He had a ski pole.

Billy's Eska had come into her own on the slippery patches. Stoical Sesi had trudged on. Five minutes ahead, and Billy'd glanced over his shoulder. Sure enough, there was the sandy-haired rival.

Then a familiar whistle, which meant, "Run faster!"

"Trail!"

Billy instructed his dogs, "Gee!" and let the challenger pass.

"Hi!" Nigel said, in his friendliest of voices.

"Hi!" Billy replied.

Soon Nigel's team were splashes of color in the distance.

Late that afternoon, Frank and Gran were bound for Yentna and the little cabin near the woods.

"Come on, Old Gal!" Frank joked to Eva, as they went along the path. It was a reference to her horse-riding days, when she was young.

For Eva, the next best thing to horse-riding was watching the sled dog teams race. They planned to take a direct route to Yentna. There was work to do, and besides, the last leg of the race was by far the most exciting!

"Ah, this is the life!" she muttered to herself as she boarded the light aircraft. The airplane taxied round to the makeshift runway, and seconds later, they were airborne.

Frank checked the altitude, and the cabin pressure. Through the port window, Eva gazed into the vast grey sky with wispy clouds, and the winter wonderland, further and further beneath them.

They landed at the little cabin near the woods. Ariana joined them. She brought her sewing with her.

Now, in the fading light, they soared over woods with snow-topped spruce, and winding paths.

Through the eyes of the artist, the trails that snaked across the wintry tundra were like threads in a giant tapestry. At intervals, trees were sewn in, stretching toward the sky. Above the snow-topped trees, a yellow-beaked eagle soared into view.

Now, the sun was sinking like a giant tangerine. Shadows loomed beneath the canopy.

Carefully, Ariana wove the threads. She wanted to show Alaska as it was, a quiet yet exciting place. Her family had belonged there for generations.

"Our lives are woven together like these threads. Yet the beauty is fragile, the future uncertain."

Ariana thought these thoughts as she glanced from the window to her work, and back again. She hand-stitched the detail of her wall-hanging. She worked from the back of the race to the front. The front runners she decided to sew last of all. They must be true to life. Her mind wandered . . .

"Who will be King or Queen Musher of them all?"

Eva, meanwhile, imagined a girl in a red cape running through the trees in daylight and at nightfall. Howls echoed through the forest. She shuddered.

*"Powdery snow floated on the air. They glided to a standstill.
The bird had landed!"*

"It's only a fairy tale, after all!"

Forty-five minutes after take-off, it was twilight. The shadowy ground loomed below them. They had flown over the mountain, over frozen swamps, rivers and lakes.

Grannie's thoughts, all the while, were never linear. They spun in spirals, in a whirligig kind of way.

Ariana dozed, clutching her sewing.

Frank had his mind fixed on the destination. They were nearly there, at Yentna station. Preparations were being made.

He turned to the women.

"Eva, Ariana! We're landing soon!"

Ariana stirred and gazed out of the starboard window. There was a picture postcard scene below them: a little log cabin half- hidden in the snow-drifts.

Frank continued the descent. The wings tilted.

The wings' metal glistened in the moist air. The undercarraige kissed the snowy earth. Shadowy snow scenes with frosted trees that seemed to shiver flashed past the side windows. The bird had landed!

CHAPTER TWENTY-TWO

The Benefactor

"Nigel's overtaken Billy!" blurted Charlie.

"So?" said Lottie, pausing at her easel.

"He's worked so hard at it. An' I feel for him! His mum's on her own. Only child. Has to take days off school as a laborer! O.K, it's not allowed. But how else can he help his mum out? But if he won—what a turn-around! Wants to be a naturalist! It's the only hope he . . ."

"What are you saying?" said Lottie, putting down her paintbrush. "I thought you were, um . . ."

"Supporting Billy?"

"Er, Yeah!"

"But he's got Jack! Jack supports both of them!"

"Who?"

"Billy and Stella, of course!"

"You're behind Stella, and so is Eva, but nobody's helping Nigel."

"But I thought you wanted Billy—then, that makes it fair!"

"No, it doesn't!"

"But Billy's only got Jack!"

"No, he hasn't, he's got Tom as well!"

Laurie tut-tutted.

"Support who you want! But he's a spoil sport!"

"He's just competitive! He wants it so badly!"

"And all the time, I thought you . . ."

"Ner, I'm sticking with Nigel. Well, I mean, it's a struggle for him, Lottie, and I'm gonna make sure he gets to school, come what may!"

Charlie's little clash with his wife of ten years did not trouble him. He knew her loyalties were less clear-cut than she implied.

On her easel, was a half-made picture of Stella, in a red cape. She had a look of triumph on her face.

"I love the way the cape blows in the wind!" Lottie had said as she gazed at the picture of Ariana's work-in-progress on her mobile.

" Ah! I haven't finished yet!" Ariana had replied. "I'm looking for some thread for the snow. Cream or white isn't real. There are so many reflections!"

Lottie's completed painting on the table was quite the opposite of the one she was doing at the easel. There was Sesi, pulling Billy's team, out at the front, a yard from the finish flag.

"Typical woman!" Charlie thought. *"If either of them succeed, she"ll say she picked the winner early on!"*

Then, out loud he muttered, "May the best one win!" Laurie gave him a sideways look, took up her paintbrush and carried on.

Charlie disappeared in his study, like a mole burrowing underground.

"Now, where was I?"

He typed the heading in bold italics:

"Mushing—Teamwork and Leadership Skills."

In his imagination, lessons like these, his lessons, made a difference in the world. These lessons had a practical bent that put theories to the test. They sent impressionable minds—curious minds, teamplayers, people with guts and gumption—problem solvers—out into the real world!

"My lessons tell real stories. This is how, through the example of real life role models—young dog mushers—we can change society—transform society for the better!"

He vowed to himself that whatever musher won, he would give a prize from his own hard-earned money towards their scholarship fund.

"*Nigel Stansford! I hope you will be lucky! You deserve it!*"

He pinned his lesson plan onto a corkboard with an orange drawing pin.

In his mind's eye, he imagined the Awards Ceremony.

"*Now, our next speaker is Charlie,*" the red-headed woman on The Junior Iditarod Committee announced.

"*What if my star pupil won!*"

"*Ladies and Gentlemen, Boys and Girls. What great talent in the race this year! Young people showing what they are made of—must be Alaskan gold! Congratulations to all the mushers. Conditions were hard this year, with a slower race than usual. You all did Alaska proud!*

Qualities that every musher has inspire young people all over the world! How sad if we can't keep up our traditions—dog sledding's in our blood.

What a sad day if our snow disappeared, everybody! Let's continue our efforts against Global Warming! Let's protect all our wildlife—everything Alaska has to offer for the next generation.

Long live Mushers!

But most of all, a big round of applause for our winner here—Nigel Stansford, and in second place, Billy Chapman. And the award for the kindest musher in the world goes to Stella Honor Chapman. Thanks, er everyone. Now, let's give Nigel Stansford here a round of applause!"

All this Charlie rehearsed. He polished his delivery till it was near perfect. He was ready for the Awards Ceremony. He told himself that when Nigel won, he would give him $1,000 scholarship money.

For a brief moment, Charlie felt the pain of when his father had gone, his mother's reversals of fortune—a poor widow, just when his own star was rising. At eighteen, how cruel the disappointment when he could not go to school!

Years later, after a long struggle, Charlie had entered the teaching profession. He understood what having an opportunity meant.

"On her easel, was a half-made picture of Stella, in a red cape. She had a look of triumph on her face."

CHAPTER TWENTY-THREE
The Hero

In every fairy tale, there's always a hero.

Billy witnessed what happened.

At the ravine, Nigel's sled went flying. He panicked, lost his footing. Two dogs broke free. Billy arrived on the scene, minutes later. At first, he saw only the sled, the dogs running loose.

"What's happened?"

He whistled. Nigel raised his hand. He was sprawled on the rocks, with gashes to his cheeks. He looked up at his rescuer.

"Help me!"

"Listen, Billy. Get the sword!" The thought came out of nowhere.

"Good thinking."

Billy Chapman said, "Whoa!" in a calm voice that was neither soft nor loud. The dogs understood. One foot on the brake, he reached into the secret compartment.

"Once, round your head!"

Without hesitation, without a question, Billy circled the wand. It protected him from danger.

Nigel's sled was balanced on a jutting rock . . .

Billy's first thought was to reach him.

Nigel outstretched his arm. They were fingertip to fingertip. Nigel grabbed Billy's hand, and pulled the glove.

"Eurgh! Dammit!"

He stumbled backwards and steadied himself. His eyes followed as Billy's glove plummeted, like a weight on a fishing line to the bottom.

Billy clambered down, edging sideways. This time he reached him. They made a human chain, Billy leading.

When they reached safety, Billy tied some cable. He lassoed it round the sled and looped a secure knot. Hunting with his father had come in useful.

"Hike!" Nigel ordered the dogs, releasing the brake. They hesitated. Then, the dogs pulled, and Billy pulled on the cable. The sled slowly ascended. Now, they were safely up! One of Nigel's wheel dogs, who was loose, whimpered. The lead dog, his harness broken, trembled.

These seconds seemed like minutes.

"Thanks, Billy," Nigel said, catching his breath. The boys stood together on the top ledge. Leaning forward, as if to question a long held opinion, Nigel searched Billy's face.

"No problem!" Billy, said. He blushed, shifted his weight from his left foot to his right.

He made a sling for the injured dog with the arm of his shirt. Together, with their repair kits, the boys made good the broken harness. When they were done, Billy said casually, "You O.K to, er, carry on?"

"Yeah, sure!" Nigel said, gathering himself together. He cradled the injured dog. "That was close!" he added, laughing.

Billy took Nigel's hurt dog; there was room in his dog bag.

Nigel stowed his lead dog. He put a team dog at the front. For a few seconds, he stared into the emptiness.

He heard voices, not far behind him.

"Ready?" he said, at last. Stella and Frances, mushers 7 and 10, were closing in.

Billy nodded.

"All Right!"

"Let's Go!"

They continued on their journey. Nigel never looked back.

The teams went through the second checkpoint.

"Best to drop this one at Yentna," the veterinary surgeon said, looking stern. Nigel nodded. *"One dog down,"* he thought. It was a challenge. But he remembered his promise to himself.

At the third checkpoint, Mrs. Jenkins, a seasoned veterinary, confirmed Nigel's dog unfit to race. Billy's team passed with flying colors. How proud he felt of Sesi! She'd come through for him!

Stella followed them. The officials waved her on. She felt relief, sighting Billy in the distance. What had happened? She'd soon know. After Yentna, things would improve! The next stage of the trail took them back the way they had come, but the final stretch was a homecoming, a familiar friend.

CHAPTER TWENTY-FOUR

Yentna Station

When Frank, Eva, Ariana, Tag and Black-Claw arrived at Yentna, crowds swarmed the bustling station. All along the river, snow-machiners had set up bonfires. In the semi-darkness against the snow, they glowed: fire and ice. Mushing fans kept vigil and cheered the racers as they flew past.

Frank's priority was to head for the log cabin. Candy glimpsed him from the window, and rushed to greet him.

"Dad!"

She ran across the snow into his open arms.

"Busy, eh? Somethin' good's cookin'!"

"Spaghetti, and burgers. 'N real coffee!"

"Best burgers for miles around!" Frank said smacking his lips. "But, Candy, first things first," Frank continued, pulling his hoodie closer to his face, "I need some help!"

Candy went back inside. With a sweet smile, her blonde pigtails swinging, the mission was accomplished with aplomb. Two boys elbowed each other in the scramble to be chosen.

Minutes later, the two young lads, in thick grey winter coats and snow-shoes who'd been doing parking duties, offered to lend Frank a hand.

They collected the supplies from his airplane. They set them down in the area for mushers and their dogs.

Dottie, meanwhile, stood at the end of the trail, in her luminous jacket. She carried a torch and shone it on the ground.

A musher was coming in from the river road. Steep banks of piled snow on each side focused him. His eyes were fixed on his goal.

Children waving scarfs and banners lined the road, shouting and cheering, they were so excited.

"I hope it's Billy!" said one little boy. He had his own mushing dreams!

Jack and Tom came, just in time to witness the spectacle; paws were flying in at breakneck speed. Uphill they were running, the musher pedaling. Then the dogs slowed, and hesitated.

Watchful Dottie guided them in; they swept round the sharp right hand turn, to the halfway point.

"Is that Billy?" Tom said, his eyes panning the scene, right to left.

"No, it's the Canadian," a young lad said.

"Where's Billy, then?" Tom said. Jack shrugged.

In the crowd, a tall young woman with dark brown hair was waving the Canadian flag.

"Hoorah! It's Nigel, bib number 3!"

Nigel's mother had traveled from Canada. How proud she felt!

Stella's best friend was watching on "Race Insider." She was thrilled her fellow Canadian led. But, for Stella, she was disappointed. Still, there was time, yet. The mushers were only halfway there.

Back in Anchorage, Charlie cheered. His star pupil! How amazing was that!

"A long way to go, yet!" Lottie muttered. She began a third painting. One with a sandy-haired boy, holding a trophy. Who would win? It was anyone's guess!

Eight minutes after Nigel, there was Billy; old faithful Sesi was leading the team.

Just ahead of him, leading the way, was a raven with blue-black wings. The night had swallowed the sun, and the sky was as black as a dark velvet cloak.

Black-Claw tilted his wings, and made the sharp turn.

The Chapmans roared on Billy's arrival.

"Hey, Billy, Hey, Billy!"

But Billy Chapman's mind was on his team though his loved ones were in his heart.

He passed the checkers, who logged his time, the injured dog. The vets inspected his dogs. He went through his own musher checklist. He examined the dogs' booties, walked round his sled to check the harnesses. He looked at his jacket, smiled at the state of his odd gloves. He dropped Nigel's dog.

Nigel, the leader, had followed musher tradition; he had chopped wood with his axe, and had lit a bonfire for all the other racers. One by one, the mushers came in. They all joined him; only William, number 5, had scratched out.

Minutes away, Stella, her red cape flying, came in at a sure and steady pace.

"Go, Stella! Hey, Stella!" the girls all shouted like cheerleaders. They jumped for joy!

"I want a cape like hers," a girl, named Rosa, said to her mother. She dreamed that one day, she would run the race.

"We'll see. They make it look easy. It's harder than you think!"

"Tag, I said, Tag!"

There was the shrill sound of someone whistling.

The fox had run to meet The Girl in The Red Cape. Several yards he was running, darting in and out, alongside the sled.

When Eva stomped her foot in protest, Tag pricked up his ears. In seconds, the fox flew to her ankles, and hid.

"Now, Tag!" Eva whispered, shaking her index finger, "I'll tell you when you're needed. You can't run around! Do you hear?"

Tag searched for Billy's lead dog, and went and made himself comfortable. To any onlooker, Tag was only part-hidden. But he believed he was invisible. With his face concealed in Sesi's fur, he quite forgot—he was as bright as the color of flames!

As darkness fell at the little outpost, the mushers all gathered to feed their dogs. They heated up water, cooked dog food on their stoves—finely shredded meat with added vitamins—to give the sled dogs stamina and strength.

"There you go. Good job, Moon!" Nigel said, putting down a bowl of tasty meat broth. She'd run the race of her life!

It was Nigel's best time ever, and young Billy knew it. Change places with him? In spite of everything, he was not envious.

There was talk that Nigel had pushed his dogs to the limit. Cruel? Not Nigel, he cared for them well. But if one thing was wrong, he was a little too pushy.

"Crabbing!" said a race veteran in a low voice. The line looked ragged. Several experts had agreed.

"My dogs need to keep all their energy for the end of the race," Stella told herself with a new feeling of authority.

Round the fire, the mushers sat, eating food and drinking pop.

Billy passed Stella another helping. His gloves were odd—one blue, one red.

"So what happened?" Stella whispered, when the others were out of earshot.

"Nigel's lead dog lost her balance," Billy whispered. "I had to help him! Jupiter's not racing. But he'll be better in a while. Mercury has the all clear! Moon's leading well! No need for him to worry!"

"You O.K, Billy?"

"Do I look O.K?" he laughed.

*"Minutes away, Stella, her red cape flying,
came in at a sure and steady pace."*

Stella wanted to pull a face, instead she nodded. Even so, she was less serious. So all that was lost was a blue glove.

Darker and darker, the sheltering sky seemed to descend. The mushers took it in turns to stoke the fire. A long way off, where race-goers and stargazers stood, the aroma of firewood and food cooking drifted on the wind. They heard the murmur of voices.

Sitting in a circle, mushers were telling jokes and stories of their dogs.

"Kinguyakki likes to dance when I play my violin . . ."

All eyes were on Stella who was telling a story of her dog named after "The Northern Lights."

"Which came first, the dancing or the name?" Douglas said with a grin. Nigel's eyes flashed under his thick sandy fringe.

"I don't know, really. The dancing, I guess. The name fitted. That's why we chose it!"

Billy and Stella exchanged a glance. In one look they felt closer even than in childhood. Everything that Gran ever said or did had a magic that lasted and sustained them.

"She's a dancer, that one! Why don't we name here after The Northern Lights!"

Stella fidgeted. After all these years, she heard her Gran's voice, her Gran's words, from way back then. Only now, she realised. They took on a new significance, a new depth.

"Ah! The Northern Lights! I wonder if we will see them?"

"Cool!" smiled Frances, the girl with bib number 10. "How long have you had her?"

"Huh?"

"How long have you had her?"

Stella awoke from that Nomansland, halfway between Dreamland and The Real World.

"Seven years, now."

"What will you do when you graduate?"

*"The dogs were dozing in their straw beds, their heads
and feet wrapped warmly under their tails."*

"Don't know yet,"

And then Stella's music came; the music she heard most of all, music of waterfalls and of mountains. Music of ink-black skies. Mushing was her life!

Nigel half-smiled. How Stella's eyes sparkled in the firelight!

"I heard you play the violin very well!"

"Well, er, I play a few tunes."

Stella Chapman's voice tailed off, her red hair fell forward, screening her face.

"And you?" Billy said, diverting attention to the sandy-haired questioner. "What do you plan to do?"

Nigel went quiet.

"Anything, I guess." He threw out his arms, his palms facing upward. How would they understand? Only he had lived his life.

But Stella noticed. Although the fireglow softened his features, he was old for his years. She'd heard he loved Nature as much as she did.

How cold the night! Yet, the snow glistened. In her mind's eye, in a state of semi-consciousness, Stella saw a dreamcatcher, quivering on the wind.

A little later, at three in the morning, she was wide-awake, her eyes always looking towards her dogs.

The dogs were dozing in their straw beds, their heads and feet wrapped warmly under their tails.

Two of the dogs, Yuraria, and her grown-up pup, Mika, the lead dog, huddled together. It was minus 20 degrees and getting colder.

The mushers watched until tiredness overtook them. Huddled in thick sleeping bags, some hunkered down for the night, slept on the snowy earth. Others slept on their sleds. They were so tired. Others drifted in and out of sleep, half awake. The boy with grazes on his cheeks was snoring softly. Stella watched him as he slept. She lifted her eyes to the firmament. The skies were changing color. Billy followed her gaze. Since childhood, he was her confidante, her trusted friend.

"Go with them, Tag," Eva whispered.
"Black-Claw, you can go ahead!"

Hours earlier, Jack, Ariana, Tom, Frank and Eva had settled in their rooms at the little log cabin nestled in the woods.

Long before dawn, Eva got dressed, donned her purple cape. She turned her key, creaked the door open, crept outside. How silent it was, how still! Black-Claw fanned his wings.

Someone else stirred, scurried to the threshold and breathed in the cold night air. Liquid shadows were moving, under the trees that surrounded the trail. Eva heard the howls of wolves! "Go with them, Tag," Eva whispered. "Black-Claw, you can go ahead!"

CHAPTER TWENTY-FIVE

The Ambush!

Ahead of the mushers was a sea of snow, bordered by a deep wood that held all the mysteries of the wilderness.

"Get ready!" said King Wolf. And the pack assembled, not far from Dottie Indigo Smith, who was standing, unawares, at the forest edge.

Checkers, who were expert dog handlers, helped Nigel lift his dogs, paws above the snow, towards the sled. Nigel's new lead dog, Moon, loved the black of the night! She gave little yips of excitement. With the dogs ready, Nigel checked the harnesses, checked the brake. He released the snow hook. "Hike!" he ordered, and they were off!

Moon sprang forward, eyes glowing. Towards the trees they went, carving a trail through birch and spruce. Dottie shone the flashlight and the dogs swept round the curve into the wood.

Two minutes later, Billy set off. Next to run was Stella.

The crimson of her cape was just visible against the dark snow-tipped greenery. Slowly she exhaled and breathed in deeply. Her nerves were calmed. She was in the driving seat!

The trail grew wider, the boys were racing, faster than the wind.

Close behind them was Stella. She saw what happened.

Nigel spotted a barricade. The trail ahead was blocked. There, forming a line, shoulder to shoulder, stood the wolves!

His lead dog, Moon, swerved. And the sled took a new direction beneath the trees.

Billy hesitated. Then, he followed.

"It is an honor to win. But a greater honor to help a fellow musher!"

These words rippled through his brain.

But in a second, the wolves were advancing on him!

Eva saw this all with her sixth sense. She sent Tag a voice command. Then to Billy she said,

"The wand, Billy. Grab the wand!"

Billy reached down to the secret compartment, grabbed the stick, with the raven carving, and brandished it above his head. The wolves were unmoved. There they stood. It was ominous.

"Billy, wave the wand, three times, above your head!"

"Swish, Swoosh, Swish!" his sword cut patterns in the thin air.

The picture in Eva's distant view sharpened.

All at once, Billy's dogs were invisible! Her grandson was protected. Some power was at work. The wolves ran for cover into the trees—all except one. She came forward. Billy's dogs outran her, turning sharply up a steep bank through the trees.

Nigel was unfortunate.

"A friend of an enemy is an enemy!" King Wolf snarled. The rest of the pack were with him. They bared their teeth. Blood-curdling howls ripped through the air.

Nigel's dogs yapped and bared their teeth.

Billy caught up, the lone she-wolf behind him.

Her eyes burned like coals of fire. Bigger and bigger, She-Wolf grew in stature, until she was bigger than the King Wolf himself.

"I said, Go! Go away and leave these innocent young men alone!"

King Wolf was silent.

"The trail grew wider, the boys were racing, faster than the wind."

"All at once, Billy's dogs were invisible!"

"Tom never killed Queen Wolf. In fact, I will show you where she has gone!"

King Wolf studied the she-wolf up and down and said, "Are you my Queen of The Wolves. Is it you that I lost?"

"No," the lone wolf said in a deep, dulcet tone. But follow me, and I'll lead you to her!"

"What burning eyes you have, Mrs. Wolf!"

"All the better to see in the dark!" the lone wolf said.

"What a big nose you have!" said Prince Wolf.

"All the better to follow a scent!" the lone wolf said.

"What huge legs you have, Lone Wolf!" Billy said.

And Lone Wolf gazed into Billy's eyes, and said, "All the better to run! And I will run with the best of 'em!"

With that, she disappeared.

Nigel and Billy were all alone in the forest.

"We can say Goodbye to this one!"

"Never say never! At least let's try to complete the race!"

Billy heard the sound of wolves approaching from behind them. He turned.

"Look!" whispered Nigel. They gazed to the heavens.

Through the trees they glimpsed a mysterious black cloud. Higher and higher it climbed. And now, at one with the firmament, it was an apparition, black as the night itself, shimmering with stars that twinkled above them.

A mysterious woman appeared in the woods. A lone wolf was with her. She stood quite still, a witch in a cape of black! The boys exchanged one swift wordless glance. The expression on her face drew the boys forward. What power in her gaze! Billy and Nigel tethered their sleds in silence. Then, the woman spoke to them. Her dark voice was soft. There was something familiar about the words she spoke.

"It is an honour to win. But sometimes, a greater honor to lose!"

"Who are you?" said Billy.

"Yes!" said Nigel. "Are you friend or foe?"

The mystical woman's gaze was so gentle. She beckoned them forward. Nigel moved in closer. Billy was braver still; he stood by her.

"Look!" said the woman. "Look at the stars!" Now, the wise woman's robes shimmered in dazzling rainbow colors. This wise woman of the woods was an angel. Perhaps, she had come from the whirling skies.

Stella's black cape swirled above the canopy. The material revealed chinks of light. They were windows to another world. An ethereal music was playing all around them. The cape cast silver threads, illuminating the snowy ground.

Billy opened his mouth to speak. But the angel had disappeared.

"She stood quite still, a witch in a cape of black!"

"This wise woman of the woods was an angel. Perhaps,
she had come from the whirling skies."

CHAPTER TWENTY-SIX

What The Crowd Saw

When the wolves ambushed Stella, only special people noticed.

"A friend of an enemy is an enemy!" King Wolf raged.

Stella struggled to shout. Where was her voice? But then, she remembered Ariana's words,

"If you are in danger, Gran says, touch the silver button. You will be invisible to all but those who love you!"

She touched the button, the silver spool. It whizzed round in seconds. All at once, the sled, the dogs and Stella were lifted, skywards.

Then, the whole crowd craned their necks, up, far up.

The cape was the sky, now ink-black with mysterious depths. It twinkled with stars. From these chinks of light, windows of the firmament, trailed thousands of shimmering threads. They cast silver upon the snowy earth.

People gasped in awe. How the snow sparkled—the stars, so bright!

Ancestors gazed down on young and old, rich and poor. The sky was transformed. It was a giant dreamcatcher; there was silver in heaven for all!

At that moment, Tom looked up and sighed.

Now, Stella led on the rainbow river road.

But many people said, "Where is Stella? Ah, poor girl! What has become of her!"

A man in the crowd was looking for her. He had a bald head, concealed by a thick wool hat. He carried a camera. Here was a photo opportunity—Stella, Rookie in the lead! He wanted The Scoop!

Black-Claw, meanwhile, made good progress. At the ravine, something attracted his attention—a bright, shiny object. He picked it up in his beak. With the stars as his guide, he tilted his wings and changed direction.

Meanwhile, at the rear, mushers were bunched together. Behind them came a little stray fox, just ahead of Nigel and Billy. In and out of the trees he went. He slid down a snowy hill, skidding into the trunk of an ancient spruce. Crack! His bushy tail kindled a fire. The Northern Lights put on a magical show for all to see. Wherever the fox was dancing, friendly fires lit the skies. They illuminated the mushers' path.

"Tag! Hey Tag!"

Tag pricked up his ears, sat for a while, then, at the swish of the sled behind him, went full pelt ahead.

Billy's dogs recognized their animal friend. They yapped and barked and howled—propelled themselves forward, faster than before. In the distance, their howls seemed to find an echo in the cry of a lone wolf.

Back home, Lottie made a painting, "The Girl in The Red Cape." Stella was flying through Alaskan skies. Woods, rivers, swamps and lakes made a miniature world spinning below her. Lottie stood back, as if to see her work better. The girl had flame-red hair, and fire in her eyes. Her hypnotic gaze followed you, wherever in the room you stood.

"Pity about Nigel!" Charlie said, wandering into the kitchen to put on the kettle. "But he's only just passed the halfway point!"

Lottie stirred the paint pot of vermillion, shook her head and smiled.

"Trail!" Nigel shouted in the semi-darkness.

"Wherever the fox was dancing, friendly fires lit the skies."

The trail curved round like a bow. In an instant, he glimpsed mushers and their sled dogs, fast-moving dots in the distance. Far, far ahead was a tiny girl musher. She was flying through the snow! But he was way back this year, with Billy, his buddy, at the rear.

At ground level, the river road shone with firelight that flickered in embers until dawn. Nigel inhaled the aroma of woodsmoke.

He heard the sound of soft voices, in the distance. A dream, unspoken, was in his heart. He widened the gap, still further away from Billy.

The man with the bald head rode a snowmachine to his light aircraft. How cold the night!

"Brrr!" He put up his collar.

At daybreak, things would emerge, become clear. Stella—vanished— yet she was on a winning streak! What was the reason? There was always talk of people missing, accident and misadventure. Tales such as these, part of the mystery of The Alaskan Triangle, which seemed to grow, year on year, made front page news! Secrets would out like wolves from their lairs. He wanted The Scoop!

*"The cape was the sky, now ink-black with mysterious depths.
It twinkled with stars."*

"At the ravine, something attracted his attention—
a bright, shiny object. He picked it up in his beak."

CHAPTER TWENTY-SEVEN

Bound for The Hunter Trail

Word had travelled fast that The Girl in The Red Cape was missing! What a commotion the press made! The man with the bald head approached Jack for an interview and a photo opportunity.

"You must be very concerned about your daughter. If she is found what message do you and your loved ones have for her?"

"Ah! She's not missing, Sir! No way! We've seen her. She's flying!"

"Er, you can't mean she's way up in front? Impossible, Sir! A reliable source has informed me that Stella is missing, and all of her dogs. What's more, rumour has it that a crone, with the face of a young woman, has been sighted in the woods!"

"Ha! Someone has a good imagination. No! Kidnapped? Not my girl! She's tough! O.K, so there are some operational blips with the G.P.S system, but the last time I saw her—she was flying!"

The stocky bald man shook his head.

A junior reporter shouldered his way through the crowd and inched between Jack and him.

"I've heard that a lone wolf is on your daughter's scent! Would you like to comment, Sir, say a few words?"

He thrust a camera in Jack's face.

Jack maintained his cool. A faint suggestion of a smile played momentarily across his lips. Such superstition, such nonsense!

Tom, who was standing nearby, avoided eye-contact. He knew!

"Er, yep! She may be a Rookie, but she's got everything worked out. I mean, um, her dogs will protect her. In any event, she's got up some speed. The new sled has all the technology! If all else fails, she'll run the wolf into the ground. She knows wolves. She knows Nature! Looks like it's gonna be a good day."

As Jack spoke these words, he looked up at the sky. The dark cloak of the night that had shimmered with shooting stars, casting their silver trails on the snowy earth, had now melted, lifted, like a giant curtain. Sunlight cast gentle tendrils all around.

When Stella reached the checkpoint at Eagle Song, shadowy forms loomed behind her across the snow. She kept her face to the sun. She knew she was not alone. Invisible and keeping her distance, the lone wolf was running alongside her. Stella sensed her.

She handed the checkers her yellow log book. All the dogs were present. They were fit for the challenges ahead. The checkers swiftly waved her through. She glanced round over her shoulder. The woman musher was nowhere in sight! What a lead Stella had built!

"Not long now!" she said to herself, though even in the morning sun, the wind had a bitter chill.

Through the woods, up and down hilly slopes, Stella coaxed the dogs. She talked to them, saying their names out loud. Sometimes she pedalled, running uphill alongside the sled to help them.

Tag, the fox, meanwhile, was sleepy. At the ravine, he sheltered amongst the rocks near the snowy river and fell asleep. Billy's glove made a comfortable pillow.

On the next leg of her journey, Stella approached a vast area of flat swamps. She checked behind again. This time, she saw the figure of a girl way in the distance.

"The smooth glide of the sled as it skimmed the snow-ocean was the stroke of the bow of her violin. A melancholy music filled the air, and enveloped her. She was at one with the dogs, the sled and the Earth."

"The pack, led by King Wolf himself, were running, faster than ever, ahead of her, their howls on the wind."

The trail ahead of Stella was a vast, flat ocean of snow. And The Girl in The Red Cape hummed a tune, the one she played on the violin, in church.

Treble and bass intertwined like snow-trails in light and shadow.

Now, ahead, were tracks as far as the eye could see. They were not paw-prints of any dog. Stella was out in front, with a secret companion. The tracks were those of the lone wolf!

Inside herself, Stella felt solitary, and free. The smooth glide of the sled as it skimmed the snow-ocean was the stroke of the bow of her violin. A melancholy music filled the air, and enveloped her. She was at one with the dogs, the sled and the Earth. The bow caressed the highest sweetest note, and Stella was in rapture at Beauty.

Alone in a world, untouched, unspoiled by the hand of man, she was the first woman, a traveller to the ends of the earth—primitive, wild, a force of Nature!

The lone wolf was bound for the woods that lay ahead. The pack, led by King Wolf himself, were running, faster than ever, ahead of her, their howls on the wind.

CHAPTER TWENTY-EIGHT

Frank, Dottie, and Ariana

W hen Frank woke up, after spending the night at Yentna Station, he tapped softly on Eva's door, to check she was awake.

There was no answer, so he tiptoed to the next room, where Ariana was sleeping.

"Ariana," he half-whispered, "A- Ariana! Are you awake?"

"Wait a minute!" Ariana whispered. She put on her dressing gown, and opened the door.

Frank shook his head, "No answer!"

Ariana stifled a yawn.

"Where is she?"

"Just like Mom," Ariana said, trying to think quickly. "Ah, now, I re-member, she had some business at the community center—Willow—maybe she forgot to tell you? Knows so many folks, maybe she has a lift or something."

"Are you sure," said Frank, studying her.

"Let's go in the room. She's probably left a message. I can check to see whether her things are there."

"Tell you what, I'll call her!"

But there was no reply; Eva's line was dead.

Ariana collected the master key, made her way to Eva's room. Frank retraced his steps to the bedroom. Dottie was standing at the window, gazing at falling snow.

"Eva's missing!" Frank announced.

"Never!" laughed Dottie. "It's always a mystery with Eva!"

"Women and their secrets," Frank said to himself. Then, out loud, "You look like you are ready, my love! There's no missing you with that jacket on!"

Meanwhile, Ariana pretended to look for her mother.

Minutes later, letter in hand, she ran down the corridor and knocked.

Dottie answered.

"Look!" Ariana said. She handed Dottie Eva's note.

Dearest A,

Hope you all slept well. Got off early with Esmeralda. She's taking me to Willow. Enjoy the race! Must fly! See you all there!

Love You, Mom X

Dottie and Ariana exchanged a glance and giggled.

"There you are!" Ariana said at last. "Unpredictable she is! Too much energy for her own good at her stage in life!"

"Well," said Dottie, looking serious. "She can look after herself, I'll give her that!"

"She looks after everyone," Ariana said as they walked together down the corridor.

"Woo! It's freezing out there!"

She watched as Dottie heaved open the heavy door, stepped outside into the icy breeze, and shone her torch in the shadows.

"Be out in a minute!" Ariana said, clapping her hands together.

Secretly, Ariana was thinking things were turning out much better than she first expected. Her mother was unusual. Everything Eva did, from when Araina was very small, had a certain magic!

When the friends had cheered Billy and Stella, their favorite mushers, on their way, they stayed at Yentna Station for a few more hours.

Frank made himself at home in the kitchens, tasting the pasta and meat casseroles, making a note of the ingredients. Dottie did crossword puzzles, while Ariana sewed.

"Who's that?" Dottie asked, pointing to a musher on the wall-hanging; a story was beginning to unfold.

"It could be anyone!" Ariana mumbled. She would sew in the detail when things were more certain.

Candy came from the kitchen area, carrying white serving plates, piled high with steaming hot food. Her pigtails swang as she greeted folks, bobbed between the tables. Frank followed her, nodding his head and smiling.

"She's cooked up a treat for us!" Frank said, his eyes growing round.

"What's on the menu!"

"Roast chicken and veg!"

"I work up an appetite just watching 'em race!"

"Hope Billy and Stella are O.K," Ariana said, looking up from her work.

"Well, they have all their supplies, and plenty o' chocolate from the shop!"

"That's good!" Ariana said.

"So generous of them!" Dottie smiled.

"Yep, there's a good community spirit here!" Frank agreed. "There are no losers. I mean, it's all about participating, having fun doing what Alaskans do best!"

"Tom never wanted to race or hunt," Ariana said, looking serious.

"Well, he won't be the first, and he won't be the last! We all have things we enjoy. He's more of an artist. Now me, I never could draw to save my life! But fish! Dottie's plated up many a salmon caught by me. An' she's caught a few herself, haven't you my dear? Now, you must have an appetite. Look at her! Skinny as the day I married her!"

Frank winked and Dottie chuckled.

They all sat down at the old oak table at the far end of the room.

Candy served them and sat down last.

"Be honest now, who do you want to win?" Frank said, looking playful.

"Stella, of course, and I think she stands a good chance!"

Ariana, who had the superstitious nature of her mother, averted her green eyes. Outside, the snow swirled and danced in the wind, clinging to the trees that surrounded the little log cabin.

"They'll need a warming meal when it's all over."

"You've gone quiet!" Frank said.

"We never talk about who may win until the end!"

Dottie Indigo Smith raised an eyebrow.

"Let's change the subject!"

Nothing spoiled the mood, their mutual support of one another.

But, they all knew something they did not say out loud. Lady Luck smiled on those who worked hard. However, she was fickle mistress; anything could happen!

On the race trail, Billy was thinking exactly that. He knew a musher's honour was worth more than any win.

"There's always next year!" he told himself. The Hunter Trail to the finish was the hardest.

It took the mushers across vast lakes and through dense woods.

In the back of his mind, he worried about unknown wolves. Even in daylight, the woods were dangerous. Now, he lagged behind.

"At least I don't give up!"

CHAPTER TWENTY-NINE
The Old Hunter Trail

Jack landed his airplane at the start of The Hunter Trail. Then, he and Tom stood in the crowd, cheering through the mushers on the last leg of the race. At intervals, Jack checked his waterproof stop-watch.

The snow churned with all the traffic, had criss-cross patterns and sludge. Families came from Alaska and Canada. Some people had arrived from Europe. Light aircraft and snowmachines had brought the world and his wife!

There they stood, shuffling and stomping their boots, waving mascots, and banners, turning up their collars, closing in their Parka hoods, shouting the names of their favorites. Their patience was rewarded; at last, late in the morning, the sun squeezed through the dense white-gray Alaskan skies.

"Hike!" Stella shouted, as she stowed her log book, lifted the snow hook, and pulled away.

Mika lurched forward. For a few seconds, Desna and Yuraria, the swing dogs, were airborne. Then, they mirrored the lead dog's direction over the icy lake, pulling behind her. Team dogs, Suka and Kinguyakki, pulled together in perfect time.

Stella, The Girl in The Red Cape, was striking out on her own, a tiny figure, with titian hair, her red cape buffeting behind her like a sail.

"Look!" said a little girl with rosy cheeks in a breathy voice. "Look Mom. It's Little Red Riding Hood!"

The sled dogs pummeled the snow to the sound of yapping from the sled dogs behind them. They receded into the horizon.

The little girl's father lifted his daughter, Rosa, high above the crowd. As if by magic, Stella, at that moment, looked over her shoulder, and waved, and Rosa's face lit up.

The woman musher, Frances, was now just minutes behind. Many mushers were clustered together in the middle, Nigel among them.

Billy, a solitary straggler, brought up the rear.

It was 11.45 a.m.

"Billy at the back. Who'd ever have believed it!" Tom said.

"An' your sis in the lead. I hope she makes it! Only one other musher who's a woman!"

"Who?" said Tom, rummaging through his pockets for the race information.

"Young Frances. She has good dogs, and she's hungry! What's gonna happen is anybody's guess! What a race!"

"She's gaining ground. Where's Grandma?" Tom panned the crowd for the woman in the purple cape.

"You remember, don't you?" Jack said, grinning from ear to ear. "Her friend, Esmeralda, is flying with her to Willow. She's the dog-breeder. The one that raised Billy's Ulva!" He gave a furtive wink, and Tom nodded.

"Ah, yeah! The dark-haired woman—blue eyes. The one that used to race!"

"Exactly," Jack said, nudging Tom who straightened up and looked straight ahead.

Stella, meanwhile, was setting the pace. The snow-carpet across the ice was like The New World, a tabula rasa on which she made the very first mark. She looked over her shoulder at the trail that swept round in a curve

One small figure was close. Many minutes a way, dark figures loomed in the distance.

Ahead of her, the big white sky and the virgin land were one. For what seemed like hours, her mind drifted with the motion of the sled. The light that had seemed so gentle, now blinded her. She saw strange apparitions; snow-shadows that seemed to dance. Sometimes, she heard voices.

For what seemed like hours, with the motion of sled and dogs, she fell into semi-consciousness.

Something brushed against face. Startled, she stirred, blinked open her eyelids, stared ahead. A dark curtain lifted. Wings fanned in the mild sun. Stella's fingers tightened on the driving bow.

The dogs were running, faster than the light itself!

Black-Claw had come!

CHAPTER THIRTY

Not Far to Go!

By the time Billy reached the lake, all the others were ahead of him! Nigel positioned himself to overtake. Billy squinted into the near distance. There was the sandy-haired challenger shouting his dogs for all his worth.

"On By!" Nigel cried as he drove his sled quite close to brown-haired Douglas, who gave him a cheery, "Hi" and a wave as he thundered past.

Then, he approached the middle bunch, and disappeared amongst them, Billy was too far back to see him; he was fast!

Billy meanwhile, struggled with Ulva, one of his swing dogs. She would not steer; she was out of step, scooping snow with her snout. The other dogs joined her, dipping their noses, drinking the snow-melt.

"Whoa!" Billy commanded.

The dogs halted.

"Might as well stop," Billy said to himself.

The spectre of failure no longer worried him; he was doing his best. He reached for dog meat ice-cubes from his supply. The dogs were thirsty, and who could blame Ulva, his little wolf-dog? At least, that's what her previous owner had called her.

Wolf-dogs had fallen out of favor. People regarded them as poor team players compared to dogs. But Esmeralda had adopted Ulva way back, before wolf-dogs were outlawed, and tamed her. She gave her to Eva. Billy had her as a birthday present. He still remembered that day. She had watchful eyes. She was playful. Eva trusted this dog she had rescued to look after the children and guard the house.

"This may be her last race!" Billy said to himself.

When the dogs had their fill, he took a swig from his flask, put what remained of his food supplies in his sled, and lifted the snow hook.

"Hike!"

Now the dogs ran with perfect timing. Ahead of them, powder flew. In the distance, the front runners and the group in the middle made across the lake for a line of trees and the trail to the wood. One last lake, and they were on their way home.

Now, Billy did not mind being the last. The sun was out, warm on his back. Everything before him looked perfect! It was so serene! He had never enjoyed leading, driving his dogs to be lonely at the front. His thoughts turned to Stella—his little sis, was she still the frontrunner, ahead of Frances and her team?

Yes, Yes, she was, but only just!

When Stella left the lake she took a sharp turn. As she changed direction, she glanced back, and there she was, Frances, the young contender. But Stella knew she was minutes away; a victory was almost within her grasp.

"On By!" shouted Frances.

"Hike!" shouted Stella.

"On By!"

"Hike . . . !"

Frances was nowhere near striking distance, Stella would not give it to her. She had to earn it.

Mika surged forward, gave it all she had. Stella's team all wanted to win!

Billy meanwhile, heartened by Sesi's enthusiasm, and Ulva's new willingness, relaxed, and the dogs relaxed and put on a sprint.

Unbeknownst to Billy, at this very second, a new drama was unfolding.

The wolves were gathering in the wood!

"This is our last chance," King Wolf announced, "and we must find our Queen or make good our loss!"

His voice descended into a snarl when he mentioned, "loss," and his wolves all snarled with him.

"A friend of a friend is a friend. But a friend of an enemy is an enemy, remember?" King Wolf continued. "Get Stella and Billy. It's their brother that took our Queen away!"

"How long will it be, Your Highness," said Prince Wolf, with a swish of his tail.

"We'll take as long as it takes!" King Wolf said. His pack were the river wolves, but some wood wolves had informed him.

Fifteen or twenty minutes passed, and Stella's hoped-for win was still uncertain.

Billy shouted, "Trail" as his sled swished past Michael who was now the racer at the back.

The group in the middle stuck together, minutes apart.

"Trail!" shouted Frances, who now took the lead, overtaking Stella.

Stella managed a "Hi" and a smile, but her heart sank.

But then, the unexpected happened.

In the middle of the wood, stood King Wolf, and his voice boomed!

"Whoa!" he called. And he stood in Frances' path.

"Are you a friend or enemy?" King Wolf said.

Frances recoiled. She glanced at Stella, who had also halted, just behind her.

"I'm a friend of Stella's," she hesitated. Stella nodded.

"Ah! Ha!" said King Wolf.

"And what do you have to say for yourself?"

"We are not afraid of you, King Wolf!"

Stella touched the silver button. This time, it brought her a voice-thought. It was Eva.

"Oh Dear, my little Sagittarius! What a time for this to happen! Just when you were almost winning, eh? And only one place away, at that. Don't worry, help is coming!"

Meanwhile, panic rippled through the line of mushers—front to middle. What about the emergency signal? They waited and waited, paralysed with fear. A storm was brewing. Hail and snow blasted through the trees. It was a strange kind of dark whirlwind.

Where was Black-Claw, where was the fox in the mushers' hour of need?

Eva had summoned them? Perhaps, she had. At that moment, as if by magic, Time itself turned back.

Eva was sitting by the fire, distance-viewing. Her spirit animals, the raven and the fox, they too, were gazing into the fiery flames! Eva saw two small children, Billy and Stella, walking alone through the snowy forest. She knew they were in danger!

"I must help them!" she whispered.

At that very moment, Billy arrived. He had heard the howls of the wolves as his approached. He reached for his wand, threw the snow hook and met the enemy face to face!

A luminous green-yellow spark flashed from his wand. It stunned the wolves. Now they were weak. But how long did he have?

The mushers in the middle stood in silence, gripping their driving bows. Dogs jumped and howled, bared their teeth, flexed their claws. The wolves watched, full of menace, but kept silent.

No-one, not even the wolves, noticed Ulva, one of Billy's wheel dogs. She was chewing through her harness.

From under the thickest trees in the woods beyond came the lone wolf. Ulva ran to meet her like a long lost friend.

"A luminous green-yellow spark flashed from his wand."

"This is your Queen!" Lone Wolf announced. "The Chapman family have treated her kindly."

"Indeed they have," said Ulva, turning to King Wolf and his pack. "Remember when I lost my home, when I let you take some of the salmon from Mr. O' Reilly's shed? I had no wolf-parents to fall back on. Esmeralda helped me. Then, The Chapmans took me in, fed me with their lapdogs. Billy and Stella, the children, were very kind to me. Stella nursed me like a mother, when I was young. Billy's my owner! He's my friend, and your friend as well!"

"But you are wild, Ulva my queen!" said Wolf King, whose smile that revealed his sharp pointed teeth was now friendlier.

"Yes, I am!" said Ulva. "This'll be my last race, Billy. Can you finish without me?"

"Of course!" said Billy. "Go where you need to be. We never knew you were a wolf, believe me. Sure, we said you were a wolf-dog. Go with your pack, where you belong!"

King Wolf's eyes softened. The spell was working, and the wolves, little by little, wanted peace. How soulful those eyes that brimmed with tears as Billy took Ulva's harness, and stowed it away. Now, she was free!

But like any true wolf, King Wolf wanted to be certain. For sometimes friends were foes in disguise. Time had changed the Queen he remembered. He needed time to get to know her again.

"I'll watch and then I'll make my decision. If she knows where her den is, the heart of her family, if she has The Spirit of The Huntress, then that'll do for me."

Lone Wolf led the wolves to Willow, Ulva followed her with the pack. Some of the wood wolves were Ulva's young, happy to see their long lost mother again.

Billy and his sled dogs followed Lone Wolf. She was the trusted one. With others he was always vigilant; they had to earn his trust.

The wolves went the long way round. For it is in the nature of the wolf to be alone and hidden with their pack on their return to the den.

"What big eyes you have, Mrs. Wolf!"

"All the better to see the trail ahead!"

"What a big nose you have!"

"All the better to follow the scent!"

"And what big paws you have!"

"Well, that's because I AM a wolf at heart!"

As for Frances, she raced ahead. The sun was high and just behind her, a raven flew with wings, blue-black.

Up and down, up and down, they went. Stella got her second wind, and overtook the front runner. Away she sailed, the red cape swirling in the snowy breeze at her back.

Crowds gathered at the winning post.

Miles in the distance, images of scarlet came through the trees. The cape was Courage, Persistence. Daring. Hard Work. Love of Wild, Wild Alaska. It was the Spirit of The Hunter, The Unity of Mushers, and Respect and Kindness towards all Creatures, and our Fellow Man.

"Hoorah!" said the man who held his daughter, high, high above the crowd in the afternoon sun.

"Wow!" breathed Lottie as she gazed at "Race Insider."

"Boy, that was close!" said Jack, as Frances swept in, just behind Stella.

"Where's Billy?" two friends said, who stood amongst the roaring crowd.

"Lottie, Lottie! Did you see Nige?" Charlie said, emerging like a mole from his study.

Lottie shrugged.

"He'll be fine!" she said, flourishing her brush. She stood back to admire her handiwork, capture the gaze.

Eva arrived at Willow, and stood at the windows, just in time to see Stella's triumph.

"That's our girl!" she said, waving her hand. "Ah! The arrow of Sagittarius, eh! Right on target! Well Done!"

Ariana gazed dreamily, first at the musher who was her daughter, then back to her sewing. She put in the last red stitch.

"I bet they are hungry!" she said.

Frank was standing next to Eva, and beamed from ear to ear. His wife, Dottie Indigo Smith, had waved Stella and her champion dogs in.

"I have some news! Billy may be coming, but he's off trail, running with a pack, running with a lone wolf!" someone said.

"He'll be in, for sure!" Eva said with a slow confident smile that made her eyes twinkle.

A man was driving his snowmachine alongside the wolves—the man with a bald head, and a woolly hat that protected it from the elements. Far away he sped, into the depths of the wild wilderness.

Running in and out, in front of him, and now behind, skipped a little red fox. In his mouth was a blue glove.

Hours and hours passed. But a search party was not needed. The man with the bald head told everyone, "Billy and The Wolves are friends!"

Someone else was with them, Nigel, Billy's new found friend.

One by one, all came in. And when the wolf swallowed the daylight, the bird with blue-black wings soared high above the wilderness, carrying a star in its beak.

As darkness fell, the wolves returned to their den. Ulva, Queen Wolf, reunited with her wolf family, safe and warm where she belonged.

"Let's keep a respectful distance," Nigel said. What a thrill to see Nature first hand, what an honor and a privilege!

Billy waved. He hoped he'd glimpse the wolves again. And the friends moved on, heading for the journey's end.

Ahead at Willow, a Musher's Banquet was being made. At the range, Dottie Indigo Smith rolled up her sleeves, her daughter, Candy, at her side.

"The face of a wolf danced in the heavens."

"Stella has the prize money, and Billy, The Red Lantern!"

These words were music to Jack's ears. He hugged Stella, and Mrs. Maddox, tears in her eyes, nodded at them both.

Men, women and children, mushers, friends and families gathered at the windows, awaiting a hero's return.

A little boy cleared the glass and pointed north.

The face of a wolf danced in the heavens.

Swishing patterns on the snowy earth, a solitary sled at last came in . . .

The crowd all cheered and rushed outside to greet them. Yaps and howls punctuated the air.

The sandy-haired contender shook Billy's hand.

"Nice work, my friend!"

Dog handlers came to assist them and tethered the sleds.

Nigel pushed open the door. He panned the room for a face in the crowd. He rushed over to say a few words. The Girl in The Red Cape had soft gray-blue eyes. He was proud of her, honored to be Billy's friend.

Tom stood quite still, alone on the threshold. He tilted his ear to the wind, and sighed.

How bright were The Northern Lights, how wild the skies!

MYSTICAL SLED RIDE

Knik to Willow, the race is on,
across the Tundra, miles from home,
Girl in Red flies through the snow,
shimmering dreams of ice-rainbows.
Sinuous bodies seem to fly
like a wolf-pack going by!
How they thunder as they run
steaming fur, in icy sun.

Knik to Willow, the race is on,
across the Tundra, miles from home,
Girl in Red, how swift she speeds,
climbing mountains for the lead!
Snowy lakes, and frozen streams,
over land of Inuit dreams,
slippery trails on icy ground,
pelting paws thunder their sound!

Knik to Willow, the race is on,
across the Tundra, miles from home,
sunburst, golden, brief respite
in winter woods,
as day meets night.
Hear the music floating by,
Girl in Red soars to the sky!
Bodies, legs and lightest paws,
across the line to great applause!

Knik to Willow, now darkness falls,
see the mushers fight for all!
Persistance, courage, strength and care,
Mushers see it through and dare!
Running fast, but running late,
the world it watches, still awake.
The brightest lantern is their guide,
stars gaze down—no longer hide.

Knik to Willow, the race was on,
and now the sled dogs all are home;
meat is plenty for them all,
winners, losers, victors all.
When Northern Lights dance in the snow,
Girl in Red, just hear them go!
Howls pierce the air, like darts -
so fast they run, their beating hearts.

Suzy Davies

BIOGRAPHIES

Biography, Anna Stephan, Winner of The Junior Iditarod, 2019

Anna Stephan mushed her way to a win this year on what was her third Junior Iditarod Race. She says that the relationship between mushers and their dogs is key,

"Look after your dogs, and they'll look after you."

A keen sportswoman, in her free time Anna enjoys soccer and cross-country running. Her favorite place in Alaska is Hatcher's Pass because it is good for snow-boarding.

She also enjoys playing the violin in church.

Anna, 18, loves dog-sledding and was first inspired to compete in the sport when she got her first dog. Her father encouraged her and her sister. She says that mushing is competitive, but the mushing community are close-knit, friendly and supportive of one another. Anna has dreams of being a teacher. She plans to continue dog-sledding.

Champion Musher, Anna Stephan, and her Dog.

About The Artist and Illustrator, Michele Bourke

F rom an early age, I can remember losing myself within the pages of Enid Blyton's. "*The Folk Of The Faraway Tree.*" Later in life, on a school trip to Tate Britain, I fell in love with a painting by John William Waterhouse, 'The Lady of Shalott,' also the works of Monet and his use of colour amazed and inspired me.

I wanted to create paintings that were equally as magical, filled with colour and strong characters, but I didn't find the time until more recently, when I became quite ill with a genetic illness, to pick up some paints and brushes. Painting is my best therapy for relaxation.

I almost gave up painting at one point, until one day a well known singer commented on how beautiful my work was. He and his PA have bought paintings from me; sometimes you need just one word of encouragement to bring your self belief back.

Artist and Illustrator, Michele Bourke

About The Author, Suzy Davies

Author and Poet, Suzy Davies, was born in Reading, England. She attended Nuneaton High School for Girls and is a graduate of The University of Leicester and a postgraduate of The University of Sussex. She comes from a background in teaching and life-coaching. She started writing at the age of six, and in later years, in 2014, became a professional writer, when she published her first book.

This work, Suzy's seventh book, *"The Girl in The Red Cape,"* is a reimagining of the original *"Little Red Riding Hood"* fairy tale, written by Charles Perrault.

Suzy's story is also inspired by Hans Christian Andersen's fairy tales and it draws on the mythology of Alaskan folk tales.

"The Girl in The Red Cape" combines a modern-day fairy tale with the wonder of nature and the thrill of adventure.

When Suzy is not behind a book, she enjoys being outdoors, on one of Florida's woodland trails, by lakes or by the sea. For a change of pace, she enjoys visiting coffee shops or restaurants. She is an avid reader of books, and enjoys all kinds of music. A lover of animals and nature, Suzy likes watching TV programmes about the planet, the environment and animals. She is also keen on stargazing and dreams of visiting an observatory and of having her own telescope to watch the night skies.

An intrepid traveller, Suzy wishes to visit Alaska one day, the setting for this fairy tale.

Suzy resides in Florida, not far from Orlando and Daytona Beach, with her husband, Craig, who is a writer. Suzy and Craig have two semi-wild visitors who come into their yard—tabby cats, Cubbie and White Socks. They also see squirrels, rabbits, hares, racoons, possums, cranes, egrets, scrub blue jays, cardinal birds, owls, ravens, hawks, lizards and gopher tortoises. Their home is a nature lover's paradise.

Portrait of Author, Suzy Davies.
Drawn by Artist, Animator, Educator, Sheila Graber,
Copyright 2019.

GLOSSARY

Lead Dog—The dog that leads the dog sled team.

Swing Dog—The dog that runs directly behind the lead dog and swings the team to run round corners or curves.

Wheel Dog—Directly in front of the sled, this dog hauls the sled round corners or trees. They are the first to take the weight of the sled being pulled.

Team Dog—A dog that runs in the middle of the team.

Crabbing—When dogs run out of line due to exhaustion or sickness.

Scratch Out—When a musher decides to abandon or leave the race due to poor performance of the team or sickness of the dogs or himself that makes it impossible to continue.

Dog Bag—A bag on the sled where sick dogs can be held until they reach a drop-off point.

Driving Bow—The bow-like handle that the musher holds onto when driving the sled.

Pedaling—pushing or kicking the ground with one foot while keeping the other on the sled to help provide extra momentum for the dog team.

Gee! Turn Right!

Haw! Turn Left!

Mush! Let's Go! Hike! All commands to encourage the dogs to get going.

Trail! A request to give a musher right of way.

On By! An instruction to dogs to overtake a musher or an obstacle.

Whoa! Halt.

The Red Lantern—A Mushing Award for a musher who shows exceptional kindness and helpfulness towards his dogs and his fellow mushers.

BIBILOGRAPHY

"Wasilla teen captures Junior Iditarod title in her third try,"
Anchorage Daily News.

"Mush! Gee! Haw! What Dog Sled Commands Really Mean,"
CBS Short Docs.

"Iditarod Dream: Dusty and His Sled Dogs Compete in Alaska's Junior Iditarod," Ted Wood.

"Don's 2000 Trail Notes: Knik to Yentna Station, 50 miles."

www.nanuq-alaska.net/donbowers/pageKni.htm

"Eye on The Trail: Yentna Station Checkpoint,"
Terrie Hanke, Jr. Iditarod News.

"Eye on The Trail: Jnr, Iditarod Celebrate Success,"
Terrie Hanke, Jr. Iditarod News.

"The World's Largest Chocolate Waterfall is Right Here in Alaska and You'll Want to Visit," Carey Seward, Alaska.

Printed in Great Britain
by Amazon